Emilia

of

Ebratha

C.J. Pearce

~ Dedications ~

Firstly, for Matthew, for listening to me ramble on for hours on end about plot ideas and characters, and helping me make decisions from time to time.

* * *

For Laura, your encouraging words kept me going, I wouldn't have finished it without you.

* * *

For Holly and Amber. I hope you enjoy reading this as much as I enjoyed writing it.

Prologue

"Just as all hope appeared lost, as the darkness closed in, the four heroes banded together to end it for once and for all. Hands clasped together as they hoped for a miracle. It was at that moment they realised they could no longer wait on a miracle, they needed to be the miracle.

Strengthened, they created a beam of light so bright; beautiful; powerful.

The Nox Malum, the creatures made entirely of shadow stood nary a chance. They were forced out, banished into an eternal darkness where they would remain for all eternity.

Celebrations and parties covered the land, citizens free once more, knowing the terrors of the night were finally gone. These heroes were thanked from all over and by whomever saw them.

They worried, however, not knowing if the dark creatures could or would ever return.

With this in mind they swore to always be there to protect the people, to use the unnatural gifts they had only for good, to protect and defend the masses.

Not only would they protect their realm, but they would protect the mortal realm also, and one brave hero volunteered to travel to the mortal realm and watch over them to ensure their safety.

For all eternity.

Although she would be a goddess amongst the people of that world should they discover her, she remained hidden and was never seen nor found. There are traces of magic all across the lands that are unexplainable and often overlooked, some say that it was her doing, helping us where possible and trying to fight any darkness that would arise, whether we realised it or not. Just as the others did, she stayed true to her oath to protect this world and would do so until the end of her time."

Christine gently closed the book before placing it on the bedside table beside her, trying to be as quiet as possible. She smiled fondly at her daughter - who was trying her hardest to keep her glossy eyes open - and kissed her forehead softly.

"Goodnight, Emilia"

Rosewood Creek

Ebratha

One

Rays of sunlight fell upon Emilia's tanned skin, soaking up every drop. Mornings were her favourite part of the day, and she would share the sunrise with her mother over a cup of hot tea, preparing for whatever the day would bring.

Taking a few more minutes to appreciate the way the light covered everything in a golden hue, Emilia stood to clear the empty mugs from the outdoor table.

Emilia started to tidy up after the chaos of the previous night. The party for her seventeenth birthday wasn't huge, but it had gotten a little out of hand regardless. The empty bottles of her father's mead was a clear indicator of that.

She pulled her thick hair into a scruffy bun, securing it with a soft hair tie, like always a few curls escaping as she did so, and her day began.

Life was simple in the quaint and charming town of Rosewood Creek. Days were spent working jobs that more often than not contributed to their society whether it be raising livestock, fishing or baking. Evenings were enjoyed together, be it with friends or family, at home or at the pub.

Being born and raised here, Emilia was very familiar with the townspeople, there was very few that she didn't know, and every now and again she assisted her family at the markets, another way in which she got to know the people of her town.

Gold was a popular way of buying goods in other towns, especially in the large cities, but here in Rosewood Creek it didn't really matter all that much. People much preferred trades; a loaf of bread or two in exchange for a dozen eggs, for example. It really was more of a community as opposed to a town, they all worked together to achieve a feeling of harmony, of peace.

This day was no different, not really. Emilia had ridden down to the town centre in the early hours after finishing her morning chores at the house - helping with the livestock; cleaning and feeding.

The Warren's had a large plot of land, and the three of them maintained it together, as a family.

Christine, Emilia's mother, was a skilled gardener and they had a large amount of land dedicated to her crops. She grew mostly vegetables, just as a few others did, and it helped keep her family fed all year round, and any surplus was used for trading.

Her father, Eden, would help during harvesting, but his pride and joy was his livestock. Mostly cows, with a few pigs. They had chickens, too, but Emilia was mostly responsible for them, along with the newest addition to the family, Daisy, the goat.

Daisy followed Emilia around constantly as she completed her morning chores; cleaning out the horse stables, checking in on the animals and feeding the chickens. While the chickens enjoying their breakfast, Emilia started to scavenge for hers as she searched the coop to see which hens had laid. With a small basket in hand, she once again returned to the house to cook up a couple for her breakfast.

With a fuller belly, and the time going by, she realised she was running a little behind schedule. Emilia had always attended the morning classes at the school, and she liked the routine it gave her. Education wasn't compulsory or enforced, but was always encouraged nevertheless.

The big cities over in Aglotar often taught extensive subjects; financing, investments, literature, physics, chemistry. Or at least that was what Emilia was led to believe.

Here at the Creek's shed of a school they preferred to teach more life skills than anything else. Valuable things you needed to live, survive and thrive. Of course they still taught the basics of mathematics, science and languages, but so much more. Cooking, baking, sewing, foraging advice, how to seek fresh water and other helpful survival skills.

It wasn't uncommon for towns far away from any major cities or landmarks to take their own twist on education. Some of the things they taught in the cities just weren't practical or needed for those that lived in these small towns. However one thing that was important was always history. Ebratha had an interesting one, after all.

Two

Many years ago, the land was whole, following the leadership of Prince Grales. Not quite ready to overtake his father and seize the role of King, but he was making waves - unfortunately not always in the right places.

The young prince had a lot of strong opinions, and they were not in favour of the masses. That more often than not only benefited a small faction of people, people like him. Of course, this lead uprisings and riots - people fighting for their basic rights.

The revolution started small, but grew over the years. A leader eventually emerged; Sir Roan Demet. Roan was the peoples' choice, never raising his own rank but nevertheless, he rose. He stood up for what was right, taking action where necessary and by any means.

Eventually, Roan was as much a character as Prince Gales and the two were constantly butting heads, up to the point where The First War began.

It lasted for years upon years until both sides exhausted themselves and their options. It was a mutual agreement that the best case scenario for both sides was to simply split the lands. Even to this day, the lands remain separate.

Aglotar.

Having the Prince and his funds, this side of Ebratha grew substantially. Riches aided in the progression. Large cities were built, with buildings that appeared to touch the sky, businesses erupting to feed the ever growing capitalist economy.
Lives appeared to be much more complex in Aglotar, even now, centuries later. They were much more technologically advanced than its rival county.

Roanloch.

Named after the person that started it all - not his choosing, either. After the war, he still assisted with the running of things, but much preferred to take a back seat. He asked across the land that they elect people in which they placed their trust, people that would assist him. Roan was not disappointed.
Small towns and villagers elected mayors that would help to run the town, make negotiations with other homesteads to acquire things that the village may need. Things seemed easier this way, simpler. Eventually Roan was able to retire back to his hometown and settle down as each town became more and more self sufficient. Life in Roanloch was often peaceful, simple and easier. It always had been, and hopefully always would be.

Emilia had never been told one straight story about how the New War started, some say it is gold, others claim it to be a power battle, some people have said that it was to do with shortages with food, resources and water, and both sides were trying to get the better deal but not one person would agree.

The main takeaway she learnt was that about two decades ago, The New War was just starting, it was a slow build up and only in the last five years has it gotten to a point where both sides were progressively getting more and more violent.

Violent enough for towns even far away from big cities were forced to take safety measures for the sake of the people. It was scary, but almost everyone was used to it now that it was just a part of daily life. Then came the days where the army would pay towns a visit, on the search for new recruits to aid in the fighting.

Whilst there weren't excessive funds available on this side of the split, there was a sense of community. One that money could rarely find. New villages appeared over the years, some grew to a larger size and became more of towns, some big enough to even be seen as a city in the eyes of Aglotar.

Rosewood Creek was one of those new villages, only finding its name a few decades ago. The village was still growing, people were still finding out about it even after all these years. One of those people was Devon Wright, along with his daughter, Taylor.

Three

"You are late." A soft smile grew on Emilia's face as she heard that familiar voice. "You said you would be here at seven. It is nearly half past!" A feminine voice chirped playfully. Emilia looked up after securing her horse to see Taylor with a funny little pout on her face. Taylor was a couple of years younger than herself, and although they were nothing alike, the two had become sisters by everything but blood.

Stood there with her auburn hair in two plaits that framed her round, freckled face, Taylor couldn't help but laugh at herself, unable to take her pouting seriously. Though the two of them were technically neighbours, they were more like family.

Taylor's father had moved in some years ago after buying the small, slightly run down farmhouse next to the Warren's. Being neighbours, Christine and Eden were straight over to introduce themselves, bringing Emilia with them.

The two girls had taken to each other right away and since then were practically inseparable. They played together, learnt together and worked together - helping each other out with anything and everything. They truly were sisters.

"Oh give over, don't act like you literally haven't just got here!" Emilia joked with the younger girl, a red hue flushing across Taylor's face proved to Emilia that she was spot on with her assumption.

"Come on, let's go get some breakfast before we head to school." Taylor changed the subject away from her tardiness, not giving Emilia the chance to be right.

"I've already eaten, I'll come with though." Emilia offered. Taylor nodded, not wanting to go alone. Together they headed over to the small cafe, it was their favourite. The scent of coffee and bacon filled the air, enticing people in. Truthfully, it was the only cafe in town, but they still loved it none the less.

The bistro also served food but was never open this early, so it was really their only option besides making something themselves but the quality was always top notch. The soft warm bread was delectable and the quality of the meat couldn't be beaten - Emilia would know, as sometimes it was pork raised from her farm.

After Taylor had devoured her sandwich, they headed over to the school building together. Despite their age gap they were still in the same class - one of the things about having a smaller population was that you all learnt together. There was an early morning class for those that preferred starting their day off with a bit of learning, but also an afternoon class for those less enthusiastic about the earlier starting time. It was all very relaxed, but it suited the town this way. Regular breaks were encouraged, too, and help was always on hand for those that needed it.

Nothing about today appeared any different - they read, they wrote, they learned. Before the class was dismissed the teacher went over recent news topics, which was standard. Emilia couldn't help but feel anxious at this part. Until the day the teacher would announce that both Aglotar and Roanloch were finally at peace again, would she continue to feel this gnawing anxiety.

Alas, that was not the case today, there was very little news about the ongoing tension between the two lands. The only thing Emilia knew, is that the war was still ongoing.

Four

The midday sun was warm on Emilia's back as she rode away from the plaza of the town square. The rest of the day was hers and hers alone, and she treasured this time. There was no doubt in her mind that Taylor would be over at her house later on, after she had finished her own chores.

Emilia stroked Ghost's neck as they approached the tree-line of the forest. It was one of her favourite places, it was quiet, yet somehow full of liveliness. Ghost also seemed to appreciate the wonders of the forest.

Emilia had received the stallion as a birthday gift some years ago after her parents had deemed it time. After all, with her taking on more of the household chores it made sense for her to have a way of her own to and from the town centre by herself.

Her parents had a cart which was pulled by their own steed, Pecan. He was getting on in years, but he had a large build that was perfect for pulling the cart that they loaded their trades on. A job that one day, Ghost would take over.

Emilia had admired his dusty grey coat with the wisps of white throughout it almost instantly. It was safe to say that he suited his name. The two of them bonded very quickly, setting their relationship off to a wonderful start which has simply strengthened throughout the years.

Emilia took a deep breath of the fresh forest air, taking in the beauty of her surroundings. Lush green bushes spread between strong, sturdy trees. The earth was soft beneath Ghost's hooves, it had rained recently, giving the trees and ferns a boost in their vibrancy and life.

The wildlife always left her feeling better about things. She was often joined by Taylor, who would happily sit quietly and sketch any of the lovely creatures they found. Her sketchbook was always brimming with pictures of the squirrels, birds, insects and even the deer that sometimes braved out into the woods.

Emilia often envied her talent, but she wouldn't want it any other way. She was happy with herself and her life, her mother was currently teaching her how to crochet, often bringing home a new yarn of wool to add to the collection. She didn't mind the hobby, but it wasn't her strong suit. She would much rather be helping her father on the farm, or riding Ghost through the scenery surrounding Rosewood Creek.

Though content in her quiet life, she couldn't help but wonder if there was something more. Emilia often found herself dreaming, longing for a life of adventure she had only read about. Perhaps one day she may take that step.

Finding her way into one of the clearings near the river, she pulled a book out of her bag, one of her favourite stories. Her mother used to read it to her on a night to help her sleep.

The World Beyond.

It told the tale of four heroes who saved their world, and the one Emilia lived in. Most people believed it to merely be a tale of fiction, a fairytale if you will. Emilia however, believed it to be something more. Something about the tale rang true with her.

Though there was no real, solid proof, Emilia had always felt something mystical about these woodlands. Something that their mortal realm had no real explanation for. Most pinned it down to child-like imagination and nothing more. They would have to find a new excuse soon, because she was nearing adulthood and she still found it to have a magical aura of sorts.

It was peaceful here, at the very least.

The town she was born and raised in was nothing compared to some of the others she had briefly visited on occasion with her parents, but even so, it was nice to get away from it every now and again and take in the world around her and the earth beneath her feet.

Her peaceful bliss was interrupted and cut short, however. She tilted her head to the sky as a flock of birds caused a commotion, flying off. Looking further, the forest was restless, creatures were scrambling. Frantic.

Something was wrong.

Just as the thought crossed her mind, a firm gust of wind came out of seemingly nowhere, even Ghost, who was always so sure and brave, was eager to leave. Quickly calming down her stallion, she climbed up onto his back and before she had even fully grasped the reins Ghost had begun to canter away.
A strange feeling had come over her as Emilia and Ghost fled the forest.

Something was warning her.

What was the warning for though? The question gnawed on her mind as she held on tight to the reins. "Woah, Ghost! It's alright!" She tried to calm the frantic steed as he jumped over any logs and small streams that crossed his path.
Home was on the horizon as they left the darkness of the forest behind but something still didn't feel right. The light from the sun was blocked by dark clouds above, or at least she thought it was clouds. It

appeared to be more of a dark shadow encasing the town she called home.

Ghost finally slowed down as she reached her homestead and for a second, she had a chance to catch her breath. Over the heavy pants from both her and Ghost, she could hear it in the distance. Coming from the heart of the town.

Air-Raid Sirens.

Five

    Panic began to set in - there were never any drills this late in the afternoon. They would normally be around midday! Emilia's adrenaline spiked further when she realised there was another sound cutting through the air, one that was a lot closer.

    She raced into the house to pick up the ringing telephone, however, her heart sank when she heard the saddened tone of her parents.

    "Emilia! Oh thank heavens you're at home! Honey listen to us closely, we don't have a lot of time here. We don't have time to get back to the house. The whole town is being locked down and we can't leave. Get to the bunker and stay there!"

    The panicked voice of her mother came from the other side.

    "You're going to be okay sweetie, okay? We'll come and find you once this has all blown over, alright?" Emilia could hear the tears just from her mother's tone alone, and it was breaking her heart.

    "We're going to be in one of the town bunkers, love." She heard her father take over, "I don't think we'll be able to come back to the house for a while, but we'll be okay, just get down to the bunker and bolt it closed, don't open it for anyone but us. There's plenty of food, water, blankets down there, everything you need."

Her father's voice came soft, softer than he would normally be. He had always been so sure of himself and exuded confidence in anything he did. Emilia had always admired him for that. This was not one of those times.

"Emilia?" His voice brought her back to the harsh reality. All she could mutter was sound - a grunt, a hum to say she heard them and was listening to them. "We love you. We love you so much, stay safe love, and we will see you so-"

Silence.

"Dad?" Emilia managed to whisper out. "Dad? Mama?" Her voice was desperate. "Are you there?"

Nothing.

The receiver slipped from her hands, dangling a few inches from the floor. Emilia was frozen in her place, having to hold a hand up to the wall to keep herself upright. *We love you. Stay Safe.* There were a couple of bunkers across the town. They would be alright. Right? She tried to convince herself but she didn't feel too sure.

She let out a shaky breath, one she had been holding a little while. Forcing herself to snap out of the trance she had been captive in.

Besides, it was all probably just a precaution. Rosewood Creek wasn't a big town by any means, and didn't have any huge landmarks that could draw attention to themselves. Why would anyone target her little home?

She tried to talk reason to herself as she made her way out of the house. It was just in case there was some aftermath, right? Bunkers were mandatory for all towns, regardless of size or population. Especially with the war showing no real signs of ending any time soon.

Homes a little further out, like Emilia's, and even Taylor's, had small bunkers built beneath their homes, big enough to comfortably house a family or two, just in case. Emilia didn't feel in control of her body - everything was a blur as she found her way down to the underground room. Her heart raced faster than it ever had before. This is what the warning was. This wasn't a precaution. This was really happening.

Just above her she heard a panicked bleat. Her baby goat, Daisy. She was only a few months old and Emilia just couldn't help herself. Before she could even think about her actions, she was walking back up the concrete steps to grab the small animal and take her back down, after all, she wouldn't mind a bit of company, it would only take a second.

Suddenly everything went silent - or so loud that she couldn't hear anything else, she wasn't sure.

All she remembered was picking up the helpless animal and a bright blue light.

It was a blinding, astonishing shade of blue. Almost grey, not dissimilar to a steel-like colour.

That was the last thing she saw before it all went dark.

The Whispers' Facility

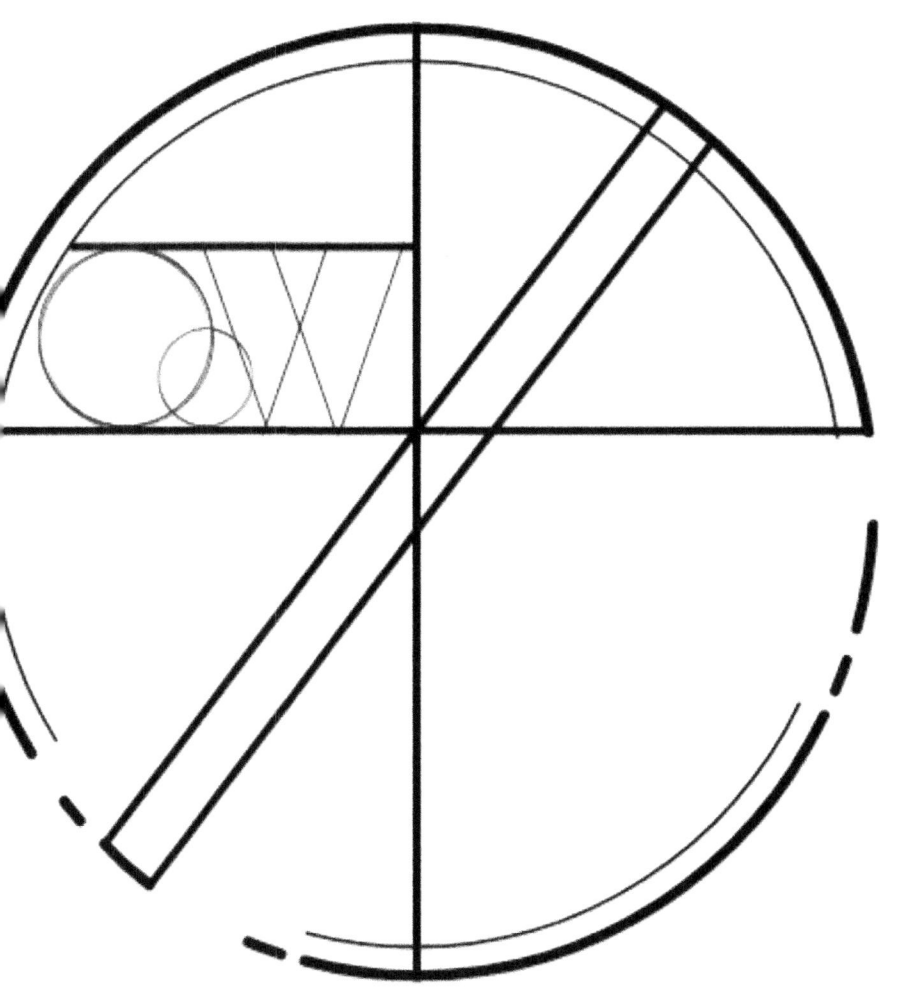

Six

It was cold.

Cold and damp.

Emilia reluctantly opened her eyes to find herself face to face with stone cold concrete. Everything hurt. Every muscle was sore, every bone ached and there was a searing pain that felt like it was ripping her head apart.

Slowly and painfully.

Putting her palms to the concrete beneath her, she tried to lift her body, but she didn't have the strength to do so. There was a muffled thud as her tired body slumped right back down.

"Woah there, take it easy." Came a gentle voice. She wasn't sure if it was in her head or not. "You've been out cold for quite some time, give yourself a minute." It came again. It definitely wasn't in her head, it was coming from beside her. It was… Kind. Something about it felt like home, yet it wasn't a voice she recognised.

Slowly, very slowly, she managed to sit herself upright. Though she did have to hold her head in her hands to stop the room from spinning. She reached to scratch an itch on the underside of her left arm, and she was met with a tight bandage, securing something in place that she doesn't remember being there before.

"It's not been in too long by the looks of it, probably best not to agitate it." She looked over to see who the voice belonged to. It was a boy, maybe a couple of years older than herself.

She studied him silently. He had dark brown hair that looked like it was just a little outgrown, a little unkempt. Almost hidden, under the dark locks, were eyes that seemed as honest as they get, they were a very light colour, kind of green and kind of grey, maybe a bit of yellow in there too, Emilia wasn't quite sure.

"I think mine itched for about two weeks straight, but it gets better."

"What is-" Emilia finally managed to speak, but it came out more hoarse than she would have liked. Her mouth felt dry, like she'd been starved of water for years. She tried to swallow, lick her lips but nothing was there.

The boy noticed and turned around, coming back in just a few seconds with a bottle of what she hoped was water, because she took it from his offered hand without hesitation.

After drinking half the contents of the bottle, she cleared her throat and tried once more. "What is it?"

"To be completely honest, I'm not entirely sure." The boy sighed, looking at his own arm, assumedly where his was. "I got told it was to keep me safe and healthy, but I don't feel any different, not really." He frowned, but shrugged, clearly trying to make it seem better than it maybe was.

"What happened? Where am I?" Emilia started to question, feeling her heartbeat start to increase. She looked at the boy for reassurance, for him to tell her it was okay. "Wait, my parents. My home. What…" She trailed off, tears starting to well in her eyes. She was scared, confused and all alone.

"Hey, hey now." That gentle tone returned, and he sat down near her, trying to make her feel at ease. "It's okay. I don't know what happened, I'm sorry." He said quietly. "But we're safe here. They call themselves the Arcane Order of Whispers and they call this place The Whispers' Facility, it's like some underground training centre of sorts. Very hush hush, hence the name."

Emilia wanted to reach out to him, she craved some kind of physical connection. She turned towards him and this was the first time she noticed the steel bars that separated them.

Her eyes shifted as she looked around, they weren't the only ones in here. There were quite a few cells of a similar size in this room, some empty, some not. Panic started to set in again.

"I don't think we're safe here. I think we're prisoners."

* * *

The next few hours were difficult. She was scared, and trapped, and she had no memory of what happened or how she got there. He was there the entire time though, trying to ease her mind. He offered her words of kindness, maybe not quite wisdom though.

He had been here a while by the sounds of it, and even though it definitely sounded like they were prisoners, it apparently wasn't all bad. Eventually, Emilia managed to regulate her breathing and calm her nerves. The residual adrenaline kept her on edge, thinking of possible ways to escape this place.

"I'm Bailey, by the way. Although I do prefer Bay, doesn't sound quite as feminine. Not that there's anything wrong with having a girly name, just… I don't feel like it suits me." He chuckled softly, still attempting to calm her down. Most of what he had been saying hadn't even been heard by Emilia, she was in such a state that she was spacing out as he talked at her, this was the first time she appeared to have acknowledged his words.

Emilia also realised this was the first time he'd even mentioned his name, and that she had been very rude and not even introduced herself to the kind stranger that had sat beside her for hours just trying to keep her calm. Taking a shaky breath as a final attempt to ease her nervous exterior, she opened her mouth to speak.

"My name's Emilia. Most people call me Emmy." She cracked a smile for the first time since she'd been here. It had been Taylor that first started calling her Emmy, and she had grown rather fond of the little nickname. Thinking about her friend didn't help though, as she started to worry about her. Had she survived?

She looked over to see Bailey smiling back at her. It was the first time she'd seen him smile too. At least she appeared to have made a friend in here if nothing else.

The two of them talked for hours, getting to know one another a little better. Emilia had never taken her peaceful life for granted before now, but hearing about Bailey's past made her treasure it just that little bit more.

Emilia had grown up with a loving family that gave her everything they could, and every chance to grow and learn. Bailey hadn't been lucky enough to encounter the same privilege.

Bailey talked about how he had grown up in an orphanage, and from the sounds of it, not a particularly good one. Even that was putting it lightly.

Emilia got the gist of it pretty early on and could tell from his body language that it was a rather touchy subject, one that she didn't push him on or pry for information. The years of abuse he endured had made him stronger it seemed though, and he appeared to be quite the protector, too.

Bailey had talked about how he did his best to stand up for the younger kids, and often took on punishments for things that weren't his fault, just so that they weren't exposed to it as early as he had been. He owed them nothing, but gave them everything he could. Emilia admired that. It was noble, and proved her earlier intuition to be correct. He was, indeed, kind.

"That reminds me," He said, a playful grin replacing the solemn look on his face. "Since you are here, it must mean you have something special about you." He was met with a puzzled look from Emilia, who had absolutely no idea what he was talking about.

"Okay, I'll go first then. The sirens were going off and the whole orphanage was being herded down to the bunker in the basement. I'm not sure if herded is the right word to use, but I know I felt like a sheep with the way they were treating us." He trailed off on a slight tangent before snapping himself back to his story.

"Anyway, so we were all heading down and before we'd all gotten down safely, the bomb had already gone off. I remember feeling like I'd been hit by a tonne of bricks. When I opened my eyes again there was burning. Things were on fire. It was an old building and things started falling apart pretty quickly.

I remember seeing Danielle next to me and this big wooden beam was falling so I did the only thing that seemed right, I tried to catch it."

He paused briefly, the look on his face made Emilia think he was reliving that moment whether he wanted to or not.

"I thought I was going to die. I thought for sure I was dead. But something changed that moment, and I was able to lift it. I saved Danielle's life that day, and she safely made it down to the bunker. So did I. Since then I've had this incredible strength.

I don't know where it came from, or why I have it. But that's what they're doing here, they're trying to work out exactly what happened. Some say it's a reaction to whatever radiation there was from the bomb, which would maybe make sense, I'm not entirely sure. Others say it's a miracle, a gift from God themself."

Bailey let out a sarcastic huff, rolling his eyes at the statement.

"I don't know why, or how, but I received a gift that day, and they're helping me make it stronger. I think the bars are to keep us safe in a way. From each other, I suppose. None of us have full control over our powers, at least not yet. They're just doing it in a very unconventional way." He paused, it was like he didn't even believe his own words, just trying to make sense out of it all.

"I'd like to say I came willingly, but it was the orphanage that let them take me. I was the only one there that was affected and from what I can assume they were given quite a large sum of gold in exchange for me." The bitterness in his voice was apparent. Being here wasn't a choice for him either, but he was clearly choosing to try and stay positive, for his own sanity. "So, what is your magical God-given gift?"

"I don't have one."

It was Bailey's turn to look confused.

"You... You don't have one?"

"No." Emilia shook her head, before stifling a small giggle at how ridiculous she was about to sound. "I tried to save my baby goat and I'm assuming that's when the bomb hit because everything went bright and then it went black, and I woke up here."

"Wait, how did you survive?"

"I don't know."

Seven

A few months had passed and no one had been able to figure out how Emilia had survived the bomb. Her and Bailey had become quite close friends, after all, they were cell neighbours.

Though, Emilia had come to the conclusion though that they were definitely prisoners here no matter how hard they tried to convince them otherwise.

They slept in their cells at night, and there were very minimal things in the cells themselves. A bed, a toilet and a sink.

Emilia couldn't understand how Bailey was still seeing the positives, especially since he had been in here longer than her, yet she admired the way he always tried to see the silver lining. It made her feel hopeful, and a little bit of hope was enough to keep her going.

When they weren't in their cells, they had guards keeping post at any doors. Making sure no one escapes. Meal times were quite bleak and it was all very basic; food that you could easily make in bulk. There was a lot of grains, beans and carbohydrates, but very little protein. It was obvious they were trying to keep costs down where possible.

They also trained for quite a large part of the day. Bailey would work on his strength and they were always pushing him for more, turning him into the fighter that everyone knew he wasn't. Bailey had made quite a lot of friends in here, and was a lot more outgoing than Emilia. She liked to keep to herself, make herself as small as possible to the point where she was mostly gone unnoticed.

Every so often though someone would break through the walls she would put up, and Emilia had grown very fond of them over time.

There was Sofia, who was able to create fire from thin air. It was very impressive, even more so after Emilia learnt about her past. Sofia had also had a traumatising experience with a burning building during the aftermath of an explosion. Her skin was permanently scorned from the flames, but it only fuelled her passion, it seemed.

Damon was able to make himself invisible, he was getting so good at it that the guards had to put a special band on him that, when activated, stopped him from being able to disappear whenever it was on him, so that he couldn't entirely vanish and disappear for good.

Then there was Isabella. She was so incredibly sweet, even her voice was sweet like sugar. Well, up until she used her powers on you. She was able to make any person tell the truth through some sort of possession. It was downright terrifying to witness.

In fact, it had been used on Emilia a few times to try and figure out what her power was, but every time it was tried on her it always ended in the same result; Emilia knew nothing.

It was clearly becoming an issue. Emilia didn't have any recollection of how she may have survived, nor was she showing signs of an ability like the others. She still trained alongside everyone else, but her training was more focused on hand to hand combat and target practice with fake replicas of the guns they used. Surprisingly, she almost felt left out when she would watch the others use their abilities in training, completing special exercises tailored to their powers.

Emilia always did as she was instructed, never caused a commotion as she never wanted to cause issues. At this point she just wanted an out, an escape. She kept on hoping that if she just did as they asked of her, an opportunity might come up with a way out of this place, but she could feel the tension constantly rising, to the point of bubbling over. She tried not to dwell on the sinking feeling, yet another intuition that something bad was about to happen.

Unfortunately, she was right.

The very next morning, even before any announcements had been made, she was roughly taken from her cell. It was an abrupt awakening, one she did not ask for nor want.

The guards weren't exactly being gentle with her either, forcibly dragging her away from the cell and towards the door. Fear may have been a part of the plan for all she knew, so she did her best to remain calm despite her racing heartbeat, but she was struggling.

She called out to her best friend in here, and she was screaming Bailey's name by the time they dragged her out of the room. She could hear his voice calling after her and the sound of metal clanging.

Before she had time to recollect herself, she was pushed into a pitch black room. There were no windows, no source of light, artificial or otherwise. It was silent here, almost peaceful. Almost.

Cautiously, she felt her way around the room, her hands moving across the stone wall. It wasn't a large room by any means, with only one door in and out. The air felt thin, like there wasn't a whole lot of it. With this in mind, Emilia did her best to steady her breathing and stay as calm as possible.

They took her into this facility for a reason, one she or anyone else hadn't quite figured out yet.

Eight

Time passed much differently in that small, dark room. Based on the meals she received, she had deciphered that she had been here for just over a week, though it felt like a lot longer.

Keeping track of her meals was the only way she could really tell. However, the longer she was kept in there, the more she felt as though she was losing her grip on reality. There was no one to turn to for advice in here, she was left alone with nothing but her thoughts and they were driving her towards insanity.

Emilia kept playing out the worst case scenario in her head, which was usually the thought that she was going to die in here, alone, in the dark and no one would know or care.

She was overwhelmed with emotions and it wasn't unusual for her to cry to the point where she was causing dehydration in herself. She started to learn to control her emotions, because she didn't have the luxury of a constant source of water, she received an allotted amount each day and that was it. The headaches that came with the dehydration weren't worth her tears.

There were days when she felt nothing but anger and would bang on the door to no end, though nothing ever came of it except exhaustion and hunger.

She learnt to overcome her frustrations in order to save her energy.

Then came the days where she felt nothing at all. She wouldn't feel tired enough to sleep away the numbness, yet wouldn't have the energy to do anything. Not that there was anything to do inside her box. It was slowly killing her.

A month, she was in there in the end. A month of eating food that was slipped through a sliding flap at the bottom of the door.

It felt inhumane, and she hated every minute of it.

One morning, whilst she was waiting for her sloppy, gruel-like porridge that they called breakfast to slide through the bottom of the door like it did every morning, something changed.

To her surprise, the entire door was being opened.

The flickering of the bulb lighting above was blinding to her, and although she knew it wasn't fresh air, it was better than what she had been breathing for the past four weeks. She inhaled deeply, taking it in.

The bliss she felt from freedom from the box was quickly short-lived as she was taken somewhere else. Exhausted, all she could do was comply and let them take her. The destination appeared to be one of the training rooms. Someone she didn't quite recognise was already stood, like he had been waiting for her.

"Alright, number thirty-seven. If nothing happens after this, you're free to go. If you survive it, that is."

Survive? She thought, trying to assess the situation before her.

There was a sound above her, some sort of alarm. It seemed to bring the other person in the room into action, as they started to run towards Emilia with a lot more energy than she could even fathom right now.

Panicked, like a deer in the headlights she froze in place, not realising what was happening.

Before she could even think about moving out of the way his fist collided with her cheekbone, the crunch of bones filling the room, quickly followed by the thud of Emilia hitting the ground. Her hand instinctively reached up to her face, she winced as she felt how sore it was.

Then… Laughter?

The guy that was in here was laughing at her. It angered her. Emilia spat out the blood that had gathered in her mouth, the red liquid vibrant against the white tiled floor. She begrudgingly picked herself up off of the floor, deciding she was not going to let this teenage boy make a fool of her. She shook some of the dust off of herself and stood with pride as she saw him work himself up for another blow.

This time, Emilia was slightly more prepared, and moved out of the way just in time. She didn't have strength on her side on a normal day, so she knew there was no point trying to beat him like that when she was devoid of all energy from being locked up in solitude for a month. However, she was small and she knew she could be quick if she tried.

She had to use her advantages wherever she could if she wanted to win this fight. Especially as it appeared the prize was her life.

As the boy moved past her, she noticed his gait was off balance thanks to the force he used to throw his fists about, and she slyly tripped him up, feeling a little better as she saw him stumble to the floor. He wasn't invincible and this was far from over.

Emilia was still trying to work out how she would be able to win this fight in her current condition, when she heard the clattering of metal.

Weapons.

They had thrown some weapons in here with them. Her heart beat rose at a rapid pace, seeing how confidently the boy picked up an axe, bloodlust in his eyes. All she could think to do was grab the first thing she saw, a dagger. She had never used tools like these before she was brought to the facility, and even now she was still getting used to them, but she definitely felt she needed something, anything, to protect herself with.

She was exhausted, she had spent four weeks with very little nourishment. The bright lights in here were giving her a terrible migraine and it was far too loud.

Every single sense was being pushed so far.

Too far.

So that when the boy approached her, she could barely even see him. She felt the pressure as he threw her against the wall, laughing again, like he was enjoying this.

The white lighting above them reflected off of the blade of the axe as he lifted it high, threateningly. Emilia's adrenaline had never been so high and something overcame her.

A bright, almost steel grey blue light, surrounded her.

With a scream of anguish, panic and fear combined, she did something she didn't know she was capable of. Without even touching the boy, she sent him, and his axe, flying across the room, straight into the stone wall and again you could hear bones splinter and crack, but this time it wasn't hers.

Panting heavily, she sank down the wall, letting her consciousness slip away once more as exhaustion finally took over.

* * *

Emilia shuddered against the cold, hard ground. Groaning as she forced herself upright. Her body ached, and her face hurt. She reached up, flinching at her own touch as she tried her best to inspect the damage to her cheekbone.

It hurt, but hurt much less now than when it happened. It didn't even feel broken. Strange, she could've sworn she heard something crack upon impact.

"Oh my god you're alive. You're okay!"

"Too loud Bailey," She grumbled, her hands going further upwards to clutch her pounding head. Not even a moment later her eyes widened and she whipped her head around, dizzying herself further in the process.

She was back in her cell. Back with Bailey and she never thought she could feel so glad while being imprisoned.

"Bailey!" She exclaimed excitedly, standing up, stumbling over her own feet as she lost her balance as she approached the bars of metal that separated them. She couldn't stop the grin from spreading across her face, though it did falter quickly.

Taking in his appearance, he didn't look too good himself. Though it had only been a month, he looked thinner, more frail than before. Weaker. He was also covered in bruises. Emilia could only assume the training was getting more intense. It angered her more than she thought it would, and she was more determined than ever to get out of this place.

"I didn't know where they'd taken you, I was so worried. What happened?" He asked, but backed down after a moment. The next words came out in a sympathetic tone. "Sorry, you must be shattered. You look like you've been to Hell and back."

"It definitely feels that way." Emilia couldn't help but chuckle lightly, and once again her lips spread into a small smile, she was happy to see him again.

"I think… I think I've worked out my power." She spoke softly, hesitantly. "I mean, I still don't understand how I did it, or what it was exactly that I did." She frowned, "But I made something happen. I felt this wave of power wash over me, and I threw this guy across the room with ease. I still passed out after, but I didn't forget anything this time. The bomb didn't cause any of the flashing lights. I remember, it was me."

Together, they tried to work out how Emilia had managed to activate her power, but nothing she did caused even a flicker of light to emit from her fingertips.

Frustrated and tired, they eventually gave up trying for the night and she filled Bailey in on the last few weeks of torture she had endured.

They discussed the possibility of her ability being adrenaline-fuelled, only appearing when she needed it most, to them it was the only logical explanation they had at this time. After all, it had only appeared both times that Emilia was in serious danger. Times where her life was at stake.

Bailey took in every word she said, and in return filled her in on things she had missed out on while being kept away. Not a lot had happened really, but strangely a few people had been going missing.

One day you'd see them, then the next they were gone. Nothing was ever said about these disappearances, and people just did their best not to pay any mind to it. It was better that way. Though since it had started happening, things had started getting stricter. There were visibly more guards around at all times, more nighttime patrols and whatever freedom they appeared to have before was long since gone now.

Eventually, they decided to truly call it a night, but it took Emilia a long time to fall to sleep. Worried that she would once again be roughly awoken, being dragged out of her cell again. Bailey did his best to ease her worries, reassuring her that she had shown them that she was capable of something, and they would probably just keep on trying to get her to grow stronger with it.

Even when she finally succumbed, it still wasn't the most restful sleep. The beds weren't particularly comfortable, and there was a constant draft that made it just a bit too cold to sleep easily.

Nine

Emilia welcomed unconsciousness with open arms when it finally came, grateful to get some rest. Her mind, however, had other ideas.

Swirls of blue and grey flooded her mind, the light some distance away. Emilia squinted, trying to make out the shape that was forming. She managed to move her feet and started to walk towards the light that appeared to be calling to her.

As she approached the light, she realised that it was in fact a body that was emitting light. Some kind of ethereal being, perhaps. She felt confused, but surprisingly not afraid. Something about the figure exuded a calm aura, and it made her feel at ease in its presence.

Emilia stood a few feet away from the being, taking in the figure in front of her. She was in awe of their beauty. The figure seemed to be floating, shrouded in the light, reminding Emilia that this was just a dream.

It was just a dream, right?

"I've been waiting for you, Emilia Lilith Warren." Her voice was soft like velvet, sending goosebumps down Emilia's skin. She swallowed nervously, not knowing how she knew her name. The being in front of her took in her body language and lowered itself onto the ground in front of Emilia, trying to ease her mind. "Oh, it's alright my dear, you don't need to be afraid. I'm glad to see you were able to wield the gift I gave you, I was a little apprehensive that it may kill you instantly."

Emilia gave her a blank look, her words sounded sinister, yet her tone was kind, happy.

"Sorry if I startled you, dear, but it was either gift my powers to you and risk it overtaking you too quickly and killing you or letting the… Gift from Aglotar kill you right there and then. So either way you would have perished…" She trailed off woefully, but perked right back up a mere few seconds later. "But you didn't! You are alive and well and fuelled with powers beyond your mortal comprehension. Oh it's all so very exciting!"

"I'm sorry. I'm struggling to keep up here." Emilia admitted, lowering the tone of the conversion. "But I keep nearly 'perishing' and to be honest I am not the biggest fan. It hurts, and I don't even know how your gift even works or what it does. I've only really managed to use it once to avoid getting an axe to the head! Is there a way for me to give you this fantastic gift back? 'Cause I don't think I want it."

The being walked closer to Emilia. Her floor length gown flowing elegantly, following her graceful movements. She placed a hand delicately on Emilia's shoulder.

"I have been watching you for quite some time, Emilia Lilith Warren. You are the one I was going to choose to receive my gift regardless, it has just happened a little sooner than intended. There are forces coming to this world that are much more dangerous than anyone in your mortal realm can even begin to imagine. Forces that almost destroyed not just my world, but all worlds.

I am not as powerful as I once was, and would not be able to return to my former glory. Unfortunately. That is why I needed to pass along my gift, to one who is worthy of it. One that would not abuse it and use it for harm. One that had a soul akin to my own. That one is you, Emilia. You may not know it right now, you might never know, but you are now a part of something greater than life itself. You, Emilia, are a protector. As a matter of fact you have been for quite some time already, you just weren't aware."

Emilia remained quiet, taking in her words, trying to understand. Though she felt nothing but doubt in her words. Emilia wasn't worthy of anything like that, she wasn't a protector of anything, she could barely protect herself. Sensing her uncertainty, the spirit smiled softly and spoke up once more.

"You will only grow stronger, my dear. You will learn in time how best to wield my gift and make it your own. I will guide you where I can, but my powers are limited now. I don't know if I will be able to reach you like this again, so I will leave you with a few words of advice. Don't be scared of it. Let it fuel you, but not overpower you, you must be in control of it at all times. Be mindful of the company you keep and how they may influence you. You are so much stronger than you realise, Emilia, and you have a full, long life ahead of you so please, live it and live it well."

The being was fading, and Emilia felt the hand slowly losing pressure on her shoulder. She shook her head, trying to stop the dream from ending.

"No, stop! Wait! I have so many questions! I don't know how to use your gift!"

"You will learn, Emilia."

"But how?" She cried out, "I don't know what I'm doing!" Emilia let out a shaky breath, she didn't have much time left and she was trying to take in everything she said whilst still trying to get some answers. "You said you might not be able to reach me, but can I reach you?"

"Perhaps, in time, my dear."

Emilia let out a groan of frustration, racking her brain for something. Her eyes lit up as she remembered something else she said. "You said you've been watching me. Are you some kind of forest spirit? In the woods near Rosewood Creek? What's your name? How can I find you?"

"Shh." The figure hushed softly. "My name is Meladia. Yes, that forest is what I call home now. You are far from your home though, but one final gift I have for you is this; Only when your time to return home comes, will you be able to find your way." With that, the figure finally faded away into the darkness, yet swirls of grey and blue remained.

Only now, they were being emitted by Emilia.

Ten

Emilia woke up in a cold sweat, dizzy and disoriented. To her surprise though, she wasn't emitting light as she was in her dream, but she definitely felt different this morning. Something had changed whilst she slept and she felt a confidence that she did not possess before. Like she was more sure of herself. Ready.

There was a lot of focus on Emilia over the next few months - after all, they had seen a small glimpse of her power and they wanted more. Just as Bailey had predicted. Training sessions were long, tiring and often brutal, but slowly, she started to get the hang of her abilities.

They had labelled her powers as telekinesis, it didn't feel quite right to Emilia - it felt like so much more than that, but she didn't want to disagree or argue with them. Her plan was to cooperate with them as much as she could in order to fly under the radar. If she caused no commotion or chaos, perhaps they would start to forget about her.

However, in the back of her mind she replayed the words of Meladia, about being mindful of the company she kept. Emilia didn't want to show these people her true strength. She wanted to master it where she could, but without giving too much away.

In time, she was able to summon her light without needing an adrenaline rush and potential danger to herself. As she was told by the spirit, she let it fuel her, but not overpower her. She soaked up the kinetic energy around her and transferred it elsewhere. Emilia didn't feel right about weaponising her gift, but the majority of her training included target practice and sparring, so it was unavoidable.

It frustrated her to no end, because she felt capable of so much more than this. This felt like what she was advised against; this was not using her gift for good. There was nothing good about destroying targets at the will of someone else and Emilia slowly started to grow resentment towards the people here. More so than she already did.

Emilia stretched out her limbs as she settled in for the night. Training was exhausting, especially on sparring days like today. Another thing she had learnt about herself and her newfound powers, were her healing abilities.

It was a little draining so she didn't do it unless she had to, but she recovered from physical injuries quicker than others, and if she chose to do so she could even focus on one particular area to almost instantly recover. It must have been why her cheekbone recovered so quickly. This was something she kept to herself, not that she'd be able to use it in target practice anyway.

She sat against the back wall of the cell while waiting for her friend. Bailey seemed to be running a little late today and a gnawing feeling in the back of her mind worried that he had become one of the disappearances. Bailey had seemed a lot more distant lately, and it hurt Emilia after all they had been through together. She tried her best not to let it bother her though, this place wasn't easy on him either.

Emilia breathed a sigh of relief when she saw him being escorted in. She looked him up and down suspiciously, he was clutching his right wrist and from the look on his face, it looked painful.

"Break or sprain?" She asked once the guards had locked up his cell and headed out. They wouldn't be back for a few hours when they came to do their lights out patrol. There was no way Bailey didn't believe her anymore about this place being a prison of sorts. What were they being punished for anyway, surviving?

"Break. I think." Bailey winced, sitting down against the back wall, adjacent to Emilia. "But they deserved it."

Emilia raised a curious eyebrow over at him, silently begging for an explanation. She bit down nervously on her bottom lip, thinking it over for a moment, but decided that she trusted Bailey enough to expose her powers to him a little more. If she was going to help anyone, it would be him.

"Bailey, give me your hand." She said to him, turning to face the bars, and holding her hands out to him to take. She was met with a look of confusion and she rolled her eyes. "I'm not asking for your hand in marriage or anything like that, you idiot. I'm literally asking you to give me your hand. Specifically the broken one."

Bailey hesitated, but he couldn't deny that he was curious as to what she was planning. So he did as she asked, and placed his hand through the bars, into Emilia's, wincing at the movement.

"I've only done this on myself before so... This could go horribly wrong, who knows." She reassured him sarcastically. She closed her eyes, as it seemed to help her focus, holding his broken wrist in her left hand and hovering her right hand above it.

There it was again, the beautiful blue light that she had grown so fond of seeing. She focussed all of her energies on his wrist, and his grunts of pain increased for a minute, worrying her that she had somehow messed up, but she pressed on regardless.

After another few minutes, the light slowly faded, dimming down to a more grey colour than blue, and even that fizzled out shortly after. Bailey looked more comfortable than he was before, but above all else he looked shocked.

He pulled his hand back through the bars to inspect it; everything looked normal. His hand wasn't glowing blue, and the pain was gone.

He applied some pressure to his wrist, expecting at least a little bit of pain, but there was nothing. Looking over at Emilia, she was nursing the same wrist that Bailey's broken wrist was on just minutes before.

"That's... New." Emilia murmured, looking confused herself, thinking out loud as she flexed her hand open and closed. "Kinda makes sense though, I guess."

"Nothing about what just happened makes sense, Emmy. What was that all about?"

"I think what you're trying to say is thank you... You know, for healing my broken wrist which now doesn't hurt anymore." Emilia retorted playfully, shaking off her wrist as the pain quickly subsided.

"I mean, yes, thank you. That feels a lot better, but are you okay? How long have you been able to do that? Is your wrist broken now or something? 'Cause I didn't agree to that, I wouldn't have let you done it if it was going to break your wrist instead!"

"Bailey, breathe, please." Emilia stated calmly. "I am fine, my wrist barely hurts, just a little twinge that will be gone in no time, trust me." She offered him a small smile. "As for your other questions, that's the first time I've done that. Well, on someone else that is. So thank you, I suppose, for being my little test subject." She laughed quietly. "But please don't tell anyone, I'm trying to keep it on the down-low, you know? After all, what good is healing when they clearly just want to turn us into weapons."

"That's exactly what they're doing. They're turning us into mindless weapons that have no other purpose but to obey."

The conversation had taken a dark turn. Neither Emilia or Bailey were smiling anymore.

"That's why people have been disappearing, if they don't respond to the conditioning after so long they just get rid of you. Or use them as target practice for the ones that do respond to the conditioning. Final test seems to be if you can kill someone on their command."

Bailey's eyes had a faraway look in them, clenching his fists instinctively. Emilia didn't have to guess that he had seen this all happen first hand.

"You attacked one of them, didn't you. One of the ones that put us in here."

Bailed nodded, a smirk spreading across his face, like he was proud about it.

"Bay, you've painted a huge target on yourself, you know they won't stand for that, right?" Emilia let out a shaky breath. "How long have you known about all of this?"

"Almost six months, but the conditioning prohibits you from talking about it outside of the rooms."

"Six months?! Bailey, I trusted you. I thought we were sticking together, you promised!"

"I didn't exactly have much of a choice, you know." His tone sounded frustrated. "Believe it or not, the conditioning isn't exactly optional. You're probably up sooner or later, you've been here, what, nearly a year now? Long enough for them to work out your strengths, weaknesses, abilities and start moulding you into a perfect little soldier for them. The shock therapy, as they call it, wasn't my favourite but I'm starting to miss it now, because it just keeps getting worse after that!"

"We have to get out of here, Bailey." Emilia tried to remain calm, and regain control of her breathing. "I knew this place was bad news from the second I woke up here, but that... That crosses the line. What you're telling me is that they're turning us into brainless killing machines with no free will." Bailey, with a look of pure defeat, just nodded. "And you've known about this for six months!"

"Getting angry at me is not going to solve anything, Emmy." Bailey retorted sharply, frustrated with her response. His own anger fizzled quickly and he let out a sigh. "Like I said, I was conditioned to not know anything about it once I was outside of the designated rooms. It's like you're in a trance and once you're out of it you have no recollection. But it's not just been going on for six months, I found my records. They've been conditioning me for two years now. They started a year after they brought me here. I've only been aware of it for six months, but even then I couldn't talk about it no matter how hard I tried."

"So how are you talking about it now, Bailey?"

"Because, believe it or not, I actually care about you enough that I am breaking that conditioning. Besides, I'm probably dead tomorrow anyway so why would they care about me anymore?"

"We need to get out of here." Emilia repeated again, trying to keep herself calm. "Don't panic."

"I'm not panicking."

"I wasn't talking about you!" Emilia snapped, raising a hand to rub her temples, the stress was taking a physical toll on her in the form of a growing migraine. "We can't just stick around and let them do this to us, it's not right. If I'd known about it sooner I would have tried to get us out a long time ago."

"I'm sorry, I wish I could have told you sooner. I just genuinely couldn't." Bailey's tone was apologetic, and Emilia knew he meant it. "But we can't do anything right now, so why don't we get some rest, and tomorrow…" His eyes met Emilia's with a seriousness she had never seen before. "Tomorrow there will be hell to pay."

Eleven

Despite there being no natural light anywhere in the entire facility, Emilia had somehow managed to get her body clock working rather well during her time here, so she woke up around the same time each morning.

Both her and Bailey had pushed their mattresses next to the bars to help them sleep a long time ago, as they often found comfort in one another - especially since they both had frequent nightmares.

There had been one night where Bailey had been inconsolable, that was the night that Emilia dragged her mattress from the table-like, rock hard bed frame, onto the ground. Bailey had done the same.

It still hadn't been enough, so Emilia sang to him that night; an old lullaby that her mother used to sing to her on days she wasn't well or couldn't sleep. It took her back to a simpler time, one she missed dearly and longed to return to.

She stretched her arms upwards as she opened her eyes, looking over towards Bailey's cell, ready to ask him what the plan was. Emilia had been a bit frantic last night, so she was hoping Bailey had come up with something, after all, he seemed to be the one that had a clear head. She could easily add to the plan and adapt where necessary, but she was struggling to think of how to start their escape.

Only one thing, though; Bailey wasn't there.

Emilia tried to swallow the lump in her throat, she hadn't heard a thing, and she wasn't exactly a heavy sleeper. There were other people awake in their respective cells, all staring at her. Was it shock? Fear? They all looked terrified of her and she couldn't understand why.

Something must have happened.

She closed her eyes, and frown lines crossed her forehead as she furrowed her brows, trying her best to think back.

Slowly, she started to remember. It was only a few hours ago, the guards had come for Bailey. They were armed and serious, knowing they were in for a fight. Bailey was probably one of the strongest people in here, Emilia had seen him in training. He wasn't one to be messed with.

Bailey was strong, but not strong enough to take on all of them all at once. They had weapons, too, of course. Bailey had nothing but his hands. He didn't go down easy, he was kicking and screaming throughout it all.

Emilia looked around again, she wasn't even in her cell, and the one next to her wasn't Bailey's. Hers was across the room, the one with no door.

Thinking again, her memory started to come back to her once more.

Emilia had ascended to another level of power as anger took over her. She had blown the metal bars clean off, and had gone after Bailey, and the guards that took him.

That's when they got her, someone had come up behind her with a syringe, injecting her with something.

Whatever it was, it had knocked her out long enough for her to be moved. Standing, she figured if she could do it once, she could do it again, right? Breaking out of this place would be a breeze with her incredible powers, she never once realised just how strong she was.

Nothing.

The door didn't budge in the slightest. She tried again, trying to focus harder this time around, but still, nothing. The third time wore her out and she dropped back down to her knees, exhausted.

Her breathing was heavy as she tried to figure everything out. Frustrated, she yelled out. No words, just a pained scream before she fell silent again, tears of anger welling up in her eyes, though she refused to let them fall.

The sound of a door opening, and footsteps approaching caught her attention.

"Now, number thirty-seven, are we done having a tantrum?" The voice was laced with sarcasm and pure evil, if evil could have a tone. She didn't respond. She refused to even look at him. "Good. I have a job for you."

A snap of the fingers and guards filled in to escort Emilia, with the big man leading the way.

He was a lanky figure, tall, with little muscle. Emilia could break him in half if she had the strength to do so right now. His face had dark shadows, though Emilia failed to understand how - he probably had a luxurious bed, the kind with duck feathers for ultimate comfort. So lack of sleep probably wasn't the reason.

She mulled it over as she followed; she was surrounded so there was very little point in fighting back now - not when she was still drained from the first injection. She needed to be patient, and strike when she was strong once more.

They led her to a familiar looking door, bolting it shut once they were all in - there were multiple locks, some electronic, some traditional. Either way, she wouldn't be able to get out.

She started to recognise the room before her; the very same place she had first learned how to use her gifts after her time in the box.

It was like a punch to the gut as she started to realise what might have been happening. The bright overhead lights were turned on, and at the other side of the room, she saw him. Stood to attention, ready to bend to their control.

Bailey.

Twelve

Emilia scanned the room hastily, she could hear words being spoken from somewhere but she was too anxious to make out what was being said. Every negative thought on how this was about to go down went through her head all at once.

There was a lovely arrangement of weapons on one side of the room, in the middle of both Emilia and Bailey. She would not be able to take him on; he was strong, she knew this from days where they would spar together in training sessions.

She also didn't wish to hurt him, he was her best friend and the closest thing she had to family, and apparently Bailey cared deeply for her too. He cared so much that he broke through whatever their conditioning was just to warn her about it.

Regret filled her body, she should have done something last night, when they had the chance. Why didn't they?

Emilia's eyes met Bailey's, and she saw the panic in them; they weren't stone cold like the last person she had been in here with.

He was scared.

Emilia started to get the feeling that he was fully conscious and would be aware of his actions, just that he would not be in control of them.

The same bell as before rang out and Bailey sprang into action, walking with purpose towards Emilia.

"Bailey," Her voice was soft, fragile. "Bailey I know you're in there. You don't have to do this. You are so much stronger than them." She pleaded, but it fell on deaf ears as he threw a closed fist right towards her.

Another skill Emilia had been developing recently was feeling how the world around her moved. It was strange at first, and often felt as though she was viewing the world in slow motion.

It was because of this that Emilia could feel the way Bailey's gait shifted as he pulled his arm back before he threw the punch. She easily shifted her own weight and avoided his fist.

He threw another.

Emilia raised an open palm, forcing his fist to change direction and miss once again without a second thought. Bailey just kept them coming, occasionally succeeding on faster blows that Emilia couldn't avoid.

"Stop!" Emilia yelled, raising both palms out towards him, forcing his whole body back a few metres, giving her a chance to catch her breath. She may have been getting used to her powers more and more each day, but it was still fairly new to her, and also still very tiring. The fact that she was still feeling the effects of whatever they injected her with wasn't helping her case.

It was a mistake, though, as she had actually pushed him towards the glistening stand of weapons, which caught his attention. Bailey's hand hovered over a few different instruments; daggers, spears, battle axes.

His hand eventually landed on the handle of a scimitar. It looked deadly, and the look in his eyes had turned dark. Whatever they had done to him, it really was working.

He stalked over to Emilia again, who knew that once again she was going to have to seriously try to defend herself. She had not even laid a hand on Bailey up until this point, she was determined not to if she could help it. She still didn't know what her limitations were or how far she could go. She didn't want to do something she would regret.

She waited for him to make the first swing, knowing that it would likely give her the opportunity to throw him off balance.

Thankfully, she was right. A quick swipe of the legs as he threw his weight into the swing of the sword and he was down on the ground.

Emilia made a break for the weapons, specifically the same one she used before. Her hand took hold of the handle of the dagger, grasping it in her right hand, pivoting to face him again. She had something to defend herself with now, something she was getting better at using too. She opted for the dagger whenever they were in training, it was the one she was most comfortable with. Small but deadly.

Bailey had used this time to get back up and take another lunge at her with his sword. She managed to move mostly out of the way, but it did get her leg on the way down. It was just like in training sessions, except this time it was serious.

Emilia kept doing all she could to not hurt Bailey, he wasn't in control of his own actions and she knew this. But she was getting tired, and bleeding from multiple wounds across her body as Bailey had landed a few more strikes of his scimitar on his intended target.

Exhausted, bloody and bruised, she didn't know how much more she would be able to take. She had to try and end this before it went too far.

She raised both hands above her head before swiftly throwing them down towards the ground, the force of her powers slammed down and rippled out.

The whole room shook, the scimitar flew straight from Baileys hand to the other side of the room, along with all the weapons so nothing was in reach.

Bailey tried lunging for Emilia again, with just his fists, but she held her hand up towards him, staring him down and using her power to hold him still, the blue light surrounding her, even her eyes lit up with the colour as she seemed to slow down time around them.

"Bailey!" She snapped, trying to catch his attention. "This isn't you, this isn't who you are!" She begged. His own eyes seemed to be shifting, like he was desperately trying to regain control of himself. "You are strong. You are so much stronger than them! You don't have to do this." She sighed, starting to admit defeat. If he had been tortured for so long to bend to their will it was futile just trying to talk him down, but she had to try.

"But, even if you can't, I just need you to know. This isn't your fault. I know it's not you. I know that this isn't who you are or what you would do. You would never hurt me. You protect, you care, you look after everyone in here, you always have and you do such an amazing job of it."

Emilia's hold on him was fading, and she was struggling. She was getting so dizzy, so faint. The loss of blood was finally catching up to her, never mind the amount of physical effort it was taking to use her powers in this way.

"It's okay, Bailey. I know this isn't you. If you're in there, though, I need you to know. I forgive you. I know you'll blame yourself for this, don't." The room was darkening at a rapid pace. "I forgive you."

The room felt as though it was spinning, the lights flickering, she knew she was losing grip. The hold she had on Bailey was gone now, so why he hadn't finished the job, she wasn't sure. Something had happened but she didn't know what. There was shouting, yelling, screaming, sirens blaring, a loud bang.

Then came the silence, the darkness. The sweet surrender of unconsciousness.

Peace.

Gold Dust Grove

Ebratha

ROSEWOOD CREEK

ROANLOCH

Thirteen

"Ow," Emilia grumbled as she regained her consciousness. "How the hell am I alive?" She muttered to herself as she managed to pull her aching body off of the ground into an upright position.

She opened her eyes to see dried blood everywhere. It was pooled around her, all up her arms, all over her clothes, simply everywhere. A normal person would have likely died from this amount of blood loss.

Not Emilia, though.

It almost felt like a recurring dream. How Emilia would wake with aching bones in an unfamiliar place, with no recollection of how she got there.

She had no idea where she was right now, though it looked to be some sort of meadow, one that appeared to be quite overgrown. She was covered in crisp, auburn leaves and yellow grass, though she didn't know why. She brushed it away from her as she tried to make sense of things, trying to remember what happened.

Her head was pounding, ringing. Dulling out any of the surrounding sounds, so she decided to stay put while she came to her senses properly, in the meantime she tried to remember what happened, try to work out how she ended up here.

The soft chirping of birds up above brought Emilia back from her thoughts. She smiled softly upon realising she really was outside, the sweet taste of freedom finally washing over her.

She could feel the warm rays of sunshine on her skin, she grasped the blood covered dirt beside her, almost in disbelief. She gasped softly when it felt real. Then came the sound of a trickle of water.

Emilia's mouth felt dry. She forced herself to her feet and followed the sound, which led her to a small stream of water.

Kneeling down at the side of the stream, she gulped down several mouthfuls, quenching her thirst.

All of those survival classes she grew up on appeared as though they would be about to help her. She rinsed off as much of the dried blood as she could, before discovering a tender spot on her arm.

As she inspected further, it was where she was implanted with that strange small device that was meant to keep them safe and healthy back at the Whispers' Facility.

Except there appeared to be nothing there anymore, and it was bandaged up with a ripped fabric, which she soon realised to be a part of her shirt.

Carefully, she took the makeshift bandage off, wincing as she looked at the mangled mess on her arm. It was gruesome, her arm had been cut up by the looks of things. She attempted to clean it, silently praying she would recover quickly and without infection. She carefully reapplied the makeshift bandage to ensure any blood remained inside her body, it looked as though she had lost enough for one day.

Wherever she was, it was alive and thriving. The wildlife seemed unaware of the perils of the world at the moment, or it just didn't care. There were plenty of insects doing their own little thing, and other small creatures seemed to be going about their day, Emilia sat for a while just watching it all.

She had seen rabbits, squirrels, a few mice and plenty of birds, too. Looking further, she even noticed a small herd of horses grazing away in the meadow.

Emilia pondered as she lay next to the stream, thinking about what her next move would be. The most logical was to follow the stream down, see if it led to any kind of civilisation.

However, the sun appeared to be much lower in the sky now, meaning it was likely going to be nightfall before she knew it. Her best bet was to try and find something to eat, do her best at purifying some water and get some rest. With her body working overtime to try and recover itself, Emilia found herself absolutely exhausted.

With this in mind, her first thought was to make a small fire, especially since the daylight was limited. Emilia wandered around the meadow to find the things she needed, trying not to head too far into the wooded area so that she didn't lose her stream.

After picking up plenty of wood of all different sizes, she headed back to the stream, wanting to stay close to it. After all, she didn't want to set fire to the meadow itself.

Emilia cleared a nice section beside the creek, flattening and clearing any grass that could potentially catch fire - she set it aside to use as tinder later if needed - and got to work on building her campfire. The last thing she needed was something to help get it going, some kindling of sorts.

Since she had been in the facility for so long she hadn't been able to keep track of the seasons, or what part of the year they were in, but she remembered how the leaves she was covered in earlier were rather on the dry side, which she could use to her advantage.

Emilia started gathering up some of the leaves that had already fallen and appeared to be dry enough, along with some twigs that she came across on the forest floor. Assuming it was probably best to get everything she needed before it got dark, because she wouldn't be able to do anything if she couldn't see.

Emilia's mind was racing, jumping from one thought to another and she was struggling to keep up. Her groaning stomach provided yet another train of thought for her; what could she eat? There were most likely fish in the river, but she knew she wouldn't be able to catch anything big without at least a net of some kind, so she would have to settle for what she could catch just with her hands.

It was much greener upstream, more plants and signs of life. Her first couple of attempts were unsuccessful, but she got the hang of it eventually and managed to catch three small fish. She didn't know what they were, but it was food that would keep her going. Trying her best to respect mother nature, she gave the fish a swift end with the help of a nearby rock.

Now all that was left was to actually start the fire and cook up her meal.

She racked her brain, taking herself back to those lessons. She needed something sharp first of all to prep her wood with, unfortunately, she didn't have anything on her, so that meant making something sharp. If only she still had her dagger. Things would be so much easier.

She found a slightly larger rock back upstream near where she had caught the fish. Emilia took the rock she had earlier and used it to knock off the edges of the larger one. It was a slower process than she had liked, and she was running out of daylight, but eventually she managed to get a relatively thin edge, like a blade.

Luckily, there were plenty of wet stones by the small river, which she used to her advantage to sharpen the edges of her rock, making it sharp enough for what she needed it for.

Returning to her little campsite, she sat down with her new blade, and removed the knobs from a long, straight stick, which she used to help her start her fire.

She rubbed her hands together, working her way down the stick, towards the flatter piece of wood it was connecting with - since she had the rock blade, she had also made dents in the flat piece of wood to keep everything in place to help with the friction.

Emilia felt as though she was trying for a lifetime, but eventually, smoke started to slither out of the wood and she sighed in relief when it began to grow and spread into a small amber flame. She gently blew towards the flame, encouraging it to grow bigger, to a point where she could add more pieces on.

Emilia now had light and heat, and she couldn't have cut it much finer if she had tried. She warmed her hands against the warm amber glow, feeling much better. She hadn't had to start a fire like that since they had done the lessons on it many many years ago. It felt like lifetimes had passed her by since then, and she felt a mournful longing for her old life.

The sharpened rock came in handy again as she prepped her dinner. Spearing the fish onto a spit that she had made. Whilst they were cooking over the fire, she made a makeshift filtering system for the river water. It wasn't her best work, and she was sure that the water close to the source would be fairly safe to drink, but she wanted to try and prevent any issues where she could.

She watched as the river water trickled through her little system, falling quite quickly through the larger rocks to be almost stopped by the sand that she had dug out of the riverbed, to eventually falling down into a little cup she had fashioned out of some of the larger leaves that she plucked from the trees.

It wasn't ideal, but it was the best she had right now.

The fish didn't taste fantastic, but it was food, and that was all she could ask for; substance to keep her going. It wasn't exactly like she had her mothers' cabinet of seasonings to her advantage right now.

Maybe, as she ventured further she might find some wild herbs, but she was far too tired for that, her body was working hard to repair itself from the action the day before. All she could do now was try to get some rest and hope that she felt better in the morning.

* * *

Dawn brought new light. A light that filled Emilia with a sense of hope. As she arose, she checked over her injuries, and just as she had hoped, they had significantly improved from the evening before. Emilia drank from her - hopefully - filtered water that was much more full now than it was before she fell asleep.

Standing, she stretched out her limbs and looked around. The small herd of horses appeared to have moved on, but the birds were up and singing, a blessing to hear after about a year of waking up to the clanging of metal doors and no natural light. She decided to stick to her plan of following the creek downstream in the hopes of finding some kind of civilisation.

Emilia followed the water source for a couple of hours before her stomach started to grumble, demanding her attention. As brutal as it had been back at The Whispers' Facility, at least there had been a constant supply of food. Out here, though she may be free, she was also all alone in the wilderness, and she was still figuring out how to survive.

Reluctantly, she wandered away from the growing riverbank into the forest that had started to surround her more and more each passing hour. Thankfully, she didn't have to go too far before she came across some sort of berry. Berries weren't the most fulfilling thing to eat, and could be risky, but after assessing the plant, its leaves and the stem, she deemed it safe to eat. She knew which kind of leaves would indicate poison berries, and these appeared to be in the clear.

They had sweet berries like these grow in the forest near her home, which were in full force during late summer, just as the nights started to last longer. These berries were a little more tart than the ones she grew up eating, but were still tasty nonetheless. She ate as many as she could see before moving on, it wasn't much, but it would do for now.

Emilia kept going, following the little river until she reached another clearing. The sunlight danced through the leaves up above, creating a lovely golden glow that kept her spirits high.

She quickly realised that not only was this a beautiful space, but also appeared to be an orchard. There were trees of different life stages, so Emilia assumed it had been well looked after, giving her hope that there was in fact some kind of town, village or settlement nearby.

She was brought back to her senses upon hearing what sounded like a stressed whinny nearby. Emilia had managed to catch up with the herd from before, and one of the horses, she noticed, was just out of reach of a delicious looking apple.

Walking over, careful not to cause a disturbance amongst the small herd, Emilia climbed up the apple tree, and knocked down a few of the ripe apples, taking a couple for herself too, before making her way back down. They were sweet, and crisp, and much more satisfying than the berries she had for breakfast.

A large mare approached Emilia, she was all black from hoof to nose, and absolutely, majestically beautiful. It looked as though it was deciding whether Emilia was a threat to her herd or not.

After a few seconds, the horse sighed gently at her in acceptance, before picking up one of the apples from the ground and moving on.

Emilia felt her body start to relax a little, she didn't mind this whole survival thing and the longer she was by herself, the more she would likely come to grips with it. Maybe she could build herself a proper little shelter for when the weather turned colder, find some plants and cultivate them here in the orchard.

Emilia felt at peace here, and the day began to get away from her, the late afternoon sun warm on her skin. She noticed that the black mare's ears were flicking back and forth a lot, as if trying to locate something. She was clearly stressed from what Emilia saw. It put her on edge, as a lot of the time animals could sense danger before humans could, and Emilia definitely trusted animals more than other humans right now.

Suddenly, the mare sprung into action, she turned towards her herd and snorted, letting them know there was danger. The horses scattered, except for the mare. She rushed over to Emilia and once again, snorted, like she was warning her of something, before trotting off to join her herd.

Emilia didn't want to hang around and find out what was going on either, so she, too, rushed into the tree line, getting out of the clearing. She wanted to be as out of the way as possible, so took it upon herself to scale one of the larger trees and hide herself amongst the branches and leaves.

It wasn't long before Emilia heard the familiar sound of hooves on ground, but also the sound of something else. It came into view not too long after she heard it, and she saw a couple of horses with carts hooked up to them.

Emilia stayed put, hesitant to approach before she knew the intentions of these people, but then she saw something that made her blood boil - two people with their wrists tied together with rope.

There was a girl, she looked like she had just entered her teenage years. She was small, though. Still so young. There was also an older female, too. She looked dazed, almost like she had been sedated at some point. She looked strong, her arms were toned with muscle and she looked bruised, as though she had put up a fight before they took them captive.

Emilia knew it in her soul that she wasn't quite ready for a proper fight just yet, she was still technically in recovery from her last one, so she had to think carefully.

It would have to be a stealth mission - there were five people, three men, two women and each of them had a blade and a gun. Those were not odds that Emilia was willing to face head on right now.

Thankfully, she still had her rock. Which, while small, if she played her cards right she would be fine with just that. Maybe if one of them was by themselves she could take them on, take their weapons and face the others. She didn't like guns, but she could easily wield the blade that they had.

Nightfall wasn't far off, and they looked as though they had decided to make camp in this clearing. They built a fire much quicker than Emilia had done the night before, but they had matches to help them start it, she did not. She could feel the warmth of the fire just by looking at it, and it made her shiver upon realising how cool it was getting now.

Once they were all settled by the fire, eating whatever stew they were cooking over it, Emilia's stomach ached once more as the smell reached her hiding space. Whilst they were all distracted by their supper, Emilia climbed down the tree as quietly as she could; being mindful of where she placed her feet and ensuring each branch she grabbed would support her weight before fully committing.

She crouched down on the ground once she reached it, making herself smaller and as invisible as she could. She could hear them laughing and talking amongst themselves so she took advantage of the noise they were making to creep around towards where the hostages were.

Emilia tried not to startle them as she approached, and once they saw her, Emilia immediately put a finger to her lips, urging them to keep quiet. They both nodded in agreement. Pulling out the sharp rock, she started to cut through the rope, again, as quiet as she could as not to draw attention to themselves.

Emilia's hair stood on end, and goosebumps started to appear on her arms, making her anxious of her surroundings. She had cut one of them loose already, and passed them the stone to cut the other loose. Emilia had a bigger issue.

From the bushes, came a petite woman, holding two daggers, poised for a fight. Emilia didn't recognise this one, there must have been a sixth person that she wasn't aware of. Slowly, she raised her arms, showing she had no weapon, maybe Emilia could reason with her.

"Let them go now, and no one gets hurt. My people have you surrounded." The woman spoke, her voice sounded a little shaky, a little nervous. There was a sweet, melodic tone to it that made it sound more like a suggestion, rather than a command.

The words confused Emilia, though.

"I was letting them go. Letting them go away from you. No one deserves to be tied up like that." Emilia retorted, her voice a bit harsher, more brash than the woman facing her.

It was the strangers turn to appear confused. She lowered her daggers ever so slightly, staring Emilia down suspiciously with eyes that reminded her of Bailey. She too had eyes that were a grey-green like colour, though more green than grey. Her heart hurt as she thought about him, still not knowing what had happened before.

Emilia had to remind herself that this wasn't him, and she was once again on edge, ready for a fight if need be.

"I think we have a couple new recruits, guys!"

Both girls turned in unison to the third voice, it was one of the men that had been just around the campfire last time Emilia checked, but the chatter must have caused a commotion, drawing the attention over to them.

Emilia was initially confused, but it didn't take long for her to realise that she was the lone wolf here. That could act as an advantage, and a means of escape, if she was quick enough.

"Fraiser." Said the young woman with the daggers, "You know why I'm here. You need to let Myla and Winnie go. They've done nothing wrong, and you know they don't have abilities. No one on this side of Aglotar does! We are so far south, so far away from Dalmaroi that none of it even matters. They are innocent."

Emilia tried to take in as much information as she

could, she recognised the name Dalmaroi, if memory serves, it was the capitol city of Aglotar. Emilia soaked up every word, hoping to slowly slink away into the darkness of the forest.

"We still have quotas to meet, Connie." The man snarked back at her, rolling his eyes, the sword in his hand still looking very relaxed, of course, he had back up if needed so it made sense for him not to be too worried, after all

"And your new friend," He gestured the sword in Emilia's direction, singling her out, ruining her plan to quietly sneak away. "Almost got away with sneaking Milo and Wynne out. If anything, you've just put them back in employment."

Smirking, he seemed very satisfied with his words. They had clearly had quite the effect on the woman - Connie, he had called her - as her body was visually a lot more tense now, she was getting angry.

"You were setting them free? My friends, Myla and Winnie." She corrected the man through gritted teeth, though he didn't seem to care either way what their names were. Emilia nodded calmly, still keeping quiet for now. Connie looked surprised at first, but then confused, suspicious even. "Why?"

Before Emilia could even open her mouth to speak, she heard an unfamiliar clicking. Both her and Connie returned their attention to Fraiser, who had put his sword away for now, and instead docked a small gun that was most definitely loaded and ready for some action.

"Now, don't get me wrong, this all very entertaining, but I was actually hoping for a nice early night and you two are keeping me up." He raised the loaded weapon, alternating his aim between Connie and Emilia, as if he was playing a game of deciding who to shoot first.

Emilia hadn't been particularly worried up until that point, but without a seconds notice, she saw one of the daggers held by Connie go soaring through the air towards Fraiser.

There was a grunt of pain, and then loud bangs, that resulted in birds taking flight nearby, scattering away frantically. Emilia sprung into action, not really noticing the pain in her abdomen.

Wincing slightly, she raced forward, diving towards the ground where one of Connie's daggers was resting on the floor after it's flight mere moments ago. Emilia was growing very fond of how light and agile they were, and the more she practiced with them, the more efficient she got.

Adrenaline was soaring through her blood, bringing her to life in an exciting way in which she least expected. Maybe a fight was just what she needed to revitalise her body.

There were others hidden away that made themselves known - Emilia quickly realised that they were with Connie, and that she hadn't been bluffing earlier. The sounds of metal meeting metal filled the air, and Emilia could smell the gunpowder from the guns.

Emilia took on each of the five, one at a time. She excelled in hand to hand combat, and she moved with grace as she wielded Connie's dagger. She felt amazing. She manipulated the world around her with her abilities, pulling and pushing her opponents with a wave of her hands, the blue light emitting ever so slightly as she showed her power to those surrounding her.

Eventually the fight was over, the quiet of the night returning. Emilia's gaze landed on the people she had just helped, hoping, praying they had good intentions. She had a good feeling about Connie, and the two that she originally set free, too. Slowly Emilia was beginning to get more in tuned with her judge of characters, and was learning what kind of people she wanted to be associated with. She wasn't sure whether her abilities helped her in that, or if it was just something she was learning with time.

Connie, Myla and Winnie, she recalled their names in her mind, were just staring at her with a look of horror. Had Emilia come across too strong? Too powerful? Had it scared them? There were two others, that she didn't know the name of. One of them looked pale, a hand over her mouth as if she was trying to hold back vomit.

"Jackson, you've got the medical supplies, right?" Connie's voice was hesitant, apprehensive. "We need to get her back home, now."

Emilia looked at them all in confusion, unsure of what the big deal was, before falling down to her knees involuntarily. When she realised what state she was in, all she could do was laugh. She was met with more distraught looks. Her hands covered her bleeding abdomen, the sight of red soaking into her hands was a sight she never thought she would get familiar with, yet here she was again, fighting for her life.

"How are you laughing right now? You've been shot, what, one, two- four! Four times!" Connie's voice came out as a screech, almost, getting quite high pitched towards the end of her sentences as she raced over to Emilia. "You are literally bleeding out!"

"Oh it's fine," Emilia laughed again, a nervous habit. "This is actually a pretty common thing for me at the moment. Don't ask."

The one Connie called Jackson swiftly approached Emilia, trying to cover the open wounds and put pressure on as many as he could.

"Don't worry, I don't think I can actually die, you know?" Delirium was taking over a little, and she giggled again. "I mean, right now I could go either way."

Everyone looked concerned, and Emilia tried to reassure them once again as they dragged her body onto one of the carts that Fraiser's group had rode in on. Emilia tried to stay conscious this time, not wanting to wake up in an unfamiliar place again, after all, she had only just become used to the new land not even two full days ago. She wasn't ready for a new place just yet.

"Hey," She heard Connie's voice above her, it was soft, but scared. "Stay with us, we're going to help. We just have a little further to go, okay."

Emilia's vision was slowly fading, though she clung on as long as she could. Connie's pleas in the background, a feeble attempt to to keep her conscious, were in vain as she let the darkness begin to take hold, to tired to hold it back much longer.

"Calm down, I already told you I'm probably not going to die." She wasn't scared anymore. It was terrifying the first couple of times, but near death experiences had appeared to be a part of her daily routine as of late. She wasn't as scared anymore.

She could hear Connie trying to reassure her, telling her that she was right, that she was going to live. That help was nearby. If Emilia could open her eyes, she would have rolled them.

If Connie had been aware of everything she had endured this past year or so, she wouldn't be as stressed, and yet, Emilia felt the sarcastic need to set the record straight before she let her consciousness completely slip away.

"*Probably* not going to die. No promises."

Fourteen

Expecting a new, unfamiliar place, Emilia opened her eyes, waiting for the dizziness that seemed to come in the aftermath.

Nothing.

No headache, no pain, no nausea.

Emilia was confused at first, and was even able to stand up right away. Had she tempted fate too much? Had she somehow managed to escape the hell that was her new reality? She took a shaky breath, and as she inhaled she could smell a mixture of fresh bread baking, earthly pine, and wildflowers, Emilia knew exactly where she was.

She was home.

Walking over the soft grass, towards the smell of freshly baked goods, she saw the little cottage she called home. Smiling softly, a wave of calmness washed over her gently.

As she reached the gate for the garden, she could see two mugs of tea on the patio table, where she used to sit with her mother to watch the sun rise before they started their day. It took her back to a simpler time, but she could also see that the liquid was hot from the steam coming from the mugs.

Curious, she took the seat that they had silently decided was Emilia's, leaving her mother's free. She reached out to grasp the mug and took a hesitant sip; it was made exactly how she usually drank her tea. It was strange yet comforting. She carefully set the mug back down.

"There you are, honey."

Tears began to trickle down Emilia's cheek in an instant. She stood up and turned towards the soft voice; her mother. Emilia fell into her embrace without a moment to lose. A gentle hand pulled her close, another softly stroking her hair to calm her.

"Oh, Emilia, it's okay, love." She soothed, "I'm here."

Emilia lost track of how long she had been holding onto her mother, but she didn't want to let go. She didn't realise just how much she missed her family.

"It's not your time yet though, sweetheart. You've got a long way to go. You're doing an amazing job though, honey, you really are."

The words that were meant to encourage her only disheartened Emilia, as she started to put the pieces together. Her parents didn't survive the attack that day. They didn't make it.

"You're not really here, are you?" Her mother sadly shook her head. "But... You feel so real. How... How are you here?"

"Someone called Meladia told me I could see you again, I had to see you, I don't know how long I'll be waiting otherwise." Emilia perked up a little upon hearing that name.

"You know Meladia? What can you tell me about her?"

"Not a lot, honey. I barely know her, she came to me and your father on the day we lost you. She wanted us to know you were alive." Her mother smiled at her proudly. "Just before she set this up, she told us what you've accomplished, my dear, and we are both so proud of you. I always knew you would be brilliant."

Emilia let out a soft laugh, it was all bittersweet.

She realised that her home was fading more and more each passing minute.

"We don't have long, do we?" She asked sadly, frowning as her mother shook her head. "That always seems to be the case."

"No, sweetie, we don't." Her mother looked to be on the brink of tears, but was holding it together for the sake of her daughter. "We love you, so very much. We can't wait to see you again, but we are happy to wait a long long time, okay honey?"

"Okay," Emilia agreed, squeezing her into another tight hug. She wasn't letting go, she refused. Slowly, everything got brighter and brighter and Emilia knew she was heading back to the real world. The dull, violent world that she was beginning to despise more and more with each passing day.. "I love you."

Fifteen

"Told you I probably wouldn't die."

Emilia croaked out as she awoke on a soft, yet firm, bed. Much nicer than regaining consciousness on the cold, hard ground that she was very well acquainted with by now. She looked over at Connie, who was writing something in a book, but quickly stopped when she realised Emilia was conscious.

"You can't stay here." Connie spoke flatly. "You are going to put my people at risk as well as yourself, and I can't have that. You need to leave as soon as you are able."

Emilia was taken aback by her stark words - she definitely had some sort of authority around here and Emilia didn't appear to be on her good side right now, though she couldn't understand why - hadn't she helped them out before?

"Sorry, hold on, you can at least tell me why. If I'm remembering last night as well as I am, I helped you and 'your people' out quite a bit last night. Or was that someone else?" Emilia retorted, frustrated that she was being pushed out without so much as a reason. Especially since they brought her here in the first place, Emilia had never asked for that.

Connie shot her a look that made her blood run cold. Those green eyes piercing her soul.

"You are not welcome here. You're one of those from The Whispers' Facility and they are nothing but bad news and troublemakers. Something you seemed all too good at last night."

Emilia was in shock, briefly speechless from sheer disbelief at the words she was hearing. She crossed her arms in disagreement. "I am *not* one of those." She snapped at the other woman, almost disgusted to be lumped in to their reputation. "I was forced in there without a choice, I was a *prisoner!* I was trapped there and treated like dirt for a year! They tried turning us in to weapons that *none of us wanted to be!*"

She could feel her voice raising and there was no stopping it. This was a build up of anger that had not had any sort of release, as Emilia had been too busy trying to survive that she hadn't actually given herself any time to process everything that had happened in such a short span of time. Before she knew it she was standing face to face with Connie.

"Unless you've actually had the absolute *pleasure* of staying at The Whispers' Facility, then you have no right to comment on the people that had no other choice but to do as they said, never mind the ones like me that somehow manage to escape that hell. Do I make myself clear?"

"Crystal." Connie smiled, closing the book. "Welcome to Gold Dust Grove."

Emilia was breathing heavily from her outburst, and was surprised that it was all over in a flash.

"I noticed the tracking chip had already been removed from your arm, I just wanted to double check what we were dealing with, and you definitely don't seem to be affiliated with them, thank goodness, because you are... Something else."

Connie carefully placed a hand on her shoulder, trying to ease her a little, Emilia instinctively flinched away from her hand.

"Hey, I'm sorry, I didn't mean to strike a nerve, are you okay, do you need a minute?" She asked, her voice sweet as sugarcane once again, Emilia wasn't quite sure which was real and which was a facade, but she definitely had a preference.

"No, I'm ok. Just confused, I think. So much has happened over the last few days, it's just... A lot." Emilia tried to pick her words carefully, not wanting to let her guard down just yet. "Water, please. Some kind of explanation would be great, too."

It didn't take long for her request to be fulfilled, she sipped carefully at the canister. It tasted as you would expect water to taste, and had no peculiar smells coming from it, so she took a leap of faith to trust them not to poison her.

"My name is Connie, by the way. Thank you for helping us last night, first of all. I know you probably don't want to hear it, but you are one fantastic fighter."

"Hm," Emilia snorted, "I'll take the compliment, thanks." After considering her options for a brief moment, and looking Connie up and down - trying to figure out any motives she may have - she decided that the truth was probably easier than a false identity. "I'm Emilia."

The notebook was back open, and Connie wrote something down that could only possibly be Emilia's name, to which she raised a questionable look towards.

"Sorry, I'm really bad with names." She let out a slightly nervous chuckle. "You did something I've never really seen before last night. You were bleeding out and we were all sure you were a goner, we got you back to camp as soon as possible, but we thought we'd lost you. Well, to be completely honest, we had lost you. You had no pulse, you weren't breathing. Officially, I think you were genuinely dead.

But then there was this light, surrounding you. I've never seen anything like it before. It lifted you from the ground and for a second I thought you were going to just ascend to the heavens or something, but after a few minutes you were brought back down and the light just vanished."

Emilia looked down at herself, and slowly started to unravel some of the bandages.

"Oh, I wouldn't do that, you were pretty badly hurt, your wounds need time to heal."

Emilia chuckled a little and ignored her advice and

continued to unravel them. There was nothing there, not even a scratch or scar. Even the larger gunshot wounds that had made large holes in her abdomen had fully recovered. The skin was slightly darker where she had been shot, but other than that there was nothing. Emilia couldn't help but wonder if Meladia had somehow helped her to heal even faster than she typically did, she brought her mother to her, who knows what else the spirit could do.

Connie was beyond surprised, she took a hold of Emilia's arm to inspect it herself, turning it over before her eyes darted further down, to Emilia's stomach that was completely fine. The woman stared in shock, taking a moment to compose herself before she tried to speak once again.

"I-" She stuttered, "I wrapped these bandages myself, you literally had holes there not even twelve hours ago!"

"Like you said, Connie, I'm something else."

* * *

Connie took it upon herself to show Emilia around. It was wasn't a big town or anything like that, it appeared to be hidden away in a shallow quarry of sorts. There was something nice about it all though, it felt like home. A lot of the facilities were mostly still just tents, with a few structures that were a bit more put together dotted around.

Emilia was given some fresh clothes that were just a little bit too big for her, but she was grateful regardless, her old clothes were torn apart and stained with blood, a mixture of her own and from others, and she was just happy to get rid. They reminded her of The Whispers' Facility, which she wanted absolutely nothing to do with.

There was a large fire pit in the centre of it all, with some pots and pans dotted around it. Emilia's stomach rumbled at the thought of a nice, hot meal, though she did her best to hide her excitement.

"Now, Myla wanted to thank you for helping us out last night and told me that you had actually already cut them free just before we got there, which I appreciate very much. She is actually a very, very skilled blacksmith, and has insisted she make you something so you have something other than a rock for future endeavours."

Emilia smiled over at the woman, Myla. She was pretty tall, which surprised Emilia a little, she had only seen her slumped over last night and didn't expect the height. Together, they designed a weapon for Emilia. It would take at least a few hours to be ready, so Connie showed Emilia around.

Jackson dealt with anything medical, so she reluctantly let him check her over, despite how Emilia insisted she was fine. He seemed very kind, he was an average height, but quite thin - potentially why he held back quite a lot during the action the previous night.

She also met with Winnie, checking to see if she was okay, she appeared to be younger than the others, but was all smiles. Emilia learnt that Winnie helped to take care of the crops and animals that the group had acquired over time with her little brother, Jamie.

Connie ran a pretty smooth operation by the looks of things too, everyone seemed to know their place here and everyone had a role. What Emilia failed to see, though, was anyone with any kind of abilities. She walked back over to Connie, sitting down next to her and clearing her throat, a little unsure of how to begin this conversation.

"So, last night, you mentioned to the Fraiser guy that no one around here has any powers or abilities, is that true?" She asked hesitantly.

"Well, it's not a complete lie. No one here at the moment has any kind of power or abilities. They often come through here to recharge and recenter themselves, before going on their way. So many have come and gone, and I don't really know much past that. I know some go to find their families, return to their hometowns, some just want to get as far away as possible."

"I remember him mention something about meeting quotas." Emilia's voice was nervous, and she wasn't sure what answer she was going to receive.

"For the agency." Connie rolled her eyes. "They have to try and recruit as many people as possible in their areas, by any means necessary. They don't realise that some of the recruiters have unconventional methods of getting people to cooperate, and if they do know about it, they clearly don't care."

"What about you?" Emilia asked in a soft tone after a moment. "You seem to be in charge around here, what's gone on here?"

"There's nothing extraordinary about me." Connie shrugged, a sad look flickering across her face. "I lost my family a long time ago, early on in this war. I've travelled about a lot but nowhere really felt like home."

Emilia gave her a sympathetic look, nothing could beat the one of a kind feeling that she knew all too well herself.

"I'm not in charge around here though, Jep is. He found me years ago, took me in. He started this place. I think it was a part of a small city before the war, there's still a few buildings hanging on. He found me hiding in one and convinced me to come with him, good thing really because a lot of those buildings have collapsed now."

"I've met quite a few of the folks around here today,

but I've not met anyone called Jep."

"Yeah, he's out on a bit of a reconnaissance mission. He's been gone a few months actually, left me in charge while he's away. Told me to keep them safe, but I don't really think I'm qualified for that. It's hard, and I don't want to let them down."

Emilia understood why Connie had appeared harsh earlier on now, she just wanted to do her best to keep everyone safe, even if that meant putting on a mask and being the tough one. She offered her a small, comforting smile.

"Sounds to me like he picked the right person."

"Miss Emilia?" Called a timid voice. Emilia, confused, looked over to the sound to see Winnie jogging over to her. "I forgot to tell you earlier! She's not one of ours, so I'm assuming she's yours. I hope you don't mind, but I've put your horse in with ours, there's plenty of food and water for her, and she seems to be getting along well with the others. Sorry, I should have told you earlier, I just got distracted."

Winnie let out a quiet giggle, giving Emilia an apologetic look, but her smile faded a little when she was met with nothing but pure confusion from Emilia.

"I don't have a horse, Winnie."

Both Emilia and Connie followed Winnie over to the stables, and once they got there, the young girl pointed over to the black mare that Emilia recognised instantly.

"She followed us when we brought you back here, so I assumed she was yours. Just made sense, you know?"

Emilia made her way over to the mare and found herself smiling as she came face to face with her again.

"What's her name? She's so pretty, and really friendly, too!" Winnie asked, as she appeared next to Emilia.

"I don't know, we only met yesterday. She's not really mine, I don't know why she followed me." Emilia thought aloud, stroking her neck softly. "What do you think we should call her?"

"Hmm, she's very pretty," Winnie stated again, clearly very fond of the horse. "Maybe we name her after a gemstone, they're very pretty too. Is there any that are black?"

"There's a couple actually," Connie chimed in. "There's Jet, but that doesn't suit her. There's also Obsidian. Oh, and Onyx, there's that one too."

The mare perked up a little at the last gem inspired name suggested, almost as in approval. Emilia couldn't help but chuckle softly.

"Onyx it is, then."

She still couldn't understand why Onyx had followed them, leaving the others behind in the process. Emilia liked to believe everything happened for a reason, and this was just another one of those things. With that thought in the back of her mind, she chose to stop trying to understand it, instead just accepting it.

The day had been rather eventful, and Emilia had learnt a lot. She could smell something cooking so she assumed it was almost time for supper. Before she joined everyone, though, she went back to Myla, to see if she could help her with anything.

Upon arrival, it appeared that the older woman had actually finished up already. She worked fast, and she produced some fantastic work from what Connie had told her. What she had made for Emilia was just another sample of her brilliance.

A sleek silver blade, glistening in the low glow of dusk. It had a gentle curve to it, and it looked deadly. The handle was beautiful, too. It was bronze in colour, with ridges to grip on to it even better.

Among the handle, you could see an intricate, delicate design that took Emilia's breath away. At the hilt, where the blade and handle met, there was a band surrounding the handle in a very familiar colour. A blue-grey colour that Emilia couldn't help but smile at in admiration.

"I admit, I may have had a bit of fun designing this beauty, she is as pretty as she is sturdy and sharp. I have no doubt you'll take good care of it."

Emilia took the blade from Myla and nodded.

"This is beautiful." She turned over the dagger in her hands, feeling the weight and how well it was balanced. She had never had something so tailored to her. "Thank you, Myla. Really."

Unable to resist the smell of food for any longer, both Emilia and Myla joined the others by the fire pit, indulging in the stew that had been simmering over the flames for some time now.

There was laughter, stories and jokes shared that evening, and Emilia felt something that she hadn't truly felt since before she received her powers. Something that had been missing in her life for a long time now. It might not last forever, for there was a lot of work to do she feared, but at least for now, for tonight.

She was happy.

Sixteen

It had been one of the most restful sleeps Emilia had experienced in such a long time. She was awoken by warm rays of sunshine heating up one half of her face. She stretched her arms out, the sleeping bag rustling at the movement. It appeared that she was actually one of the last up, everyone else had already begun their day.

"Morning, sleepy head." Connie's voice came from above her, a little more hoarse than usual it was still very early in the day. "I didn't want to overwhelm you yesterday, sounds like you've been through a lot in a pretty short space of time. But we do need to discuss it today, get some breakfast, have a coffee if need be and when you feel ready, come see me, okay?"

Emilia was left with a peculiar, anxious feeling as she watched Connie walk away from her. A part of her wanted to take Onyx and ride fast and far, get as much distance between herself and this place as possible, but something inside her knew she was needed here and that was something that she just wasn't able to walk away from, at least not just yet.

As instructed, she replenished herself, helping herself to some toasted bread with some berry preserve to add some sweetness. It balanced out the bitterness of the coffee nicely. Nerves were building, and Emilia didn't want to put it off any longer so as soon as she spotted Connie, she started to make her way over.

"All good?" Connie checked, Emilia just nodded. "Good, follow me."

She led Emilia into a tent, similar to the one she first woke up in. Inside was rather bare, with a wooden table in the middle, documents scattered atop it. Connie grabbed one from the top of the file and gestured for Emilia to come closer. Upon closer inspection, Emilia realised it was a map.

"This is our camp, here," Connie pointed out. "Now, we have been trying to locate these facilities for a long time but they're very clever and actually built underground for the most part, which makes it harder. A few weeks ago, we managed to pin point one just about here." She moved her hand to another location on the map, which had been circled.

"This is where we met you, Emilia." Connie marked a small cross about halfway between the two points. "Which would mean that it's very likely that you came from the underground facility there. At least, statistically that would make sense."
Emilia nodded in agreement.

"However, something very odd has happened very very recently. Four days ago, that facility was raided and completely destroyed. There's nothing but a hole in the ground there now where it used to be."

Nausea washed over Emilia like a wave, the ground felt as though it was collapsing beneath her and there was nothing she could do. As much as she had hated it there, all she could think about was Bailey. She tried to swallow down the lump in her throat, then her eyes finally met Connie's again as she took a deep breath.

"Will you take me there? I think I need to see it for myself."

It didn't take more than a couple of hours on horseback to reach the marked location. While it had been quite some time since Emilia had ridden, it came quite natural atop Onyx, though it didn't feel like any other horse she had ridden before.

Rubble and debris littered the landscape, scraps of metal scaffolding poking out from the ground, it looked as though someone had tried to bury this place and the horrific things they did along with it. There was no signs of life left, no sign of Bailey.

"Who destroyed it? And why?" Emilia asked as she looked back over at Connie.

"We have found some information on a growing group that are going up against the Whispers. From what we've found out so far they call themselves The Afterward Censorship Heroes. Extremely vain in my opinion." Connie stated with a dramatic eye roll, accompanied with a scoff of disapproval. "Imagine creating a rebel group and calling yourselves heroes."

"Anyways, they're growing in numbers, they're developing an agency at this point and they are trying to target any Whisper's Facilities that they are aware of. It's who Fraiser was working for and recruiting for. Clearly, they have a lot of power." Connie gestured towards the wreckage. "So they're not to be messed with, really. I try and keep a distance where I can, I don't really want to take any chances with them, I don't get a good feeling and I just can't bring myself to trust them. Especially if they work with people like Fraiser, who's morals are clearly on the floor."

Emilia had kept quiet, just listening to Connie bring her up to speed, it appears that she had missed quite a lot in the year she had been underground. It was a lot to take in, but she tried to keep up as much as possible. She realised she no longer knew what was going on - was there even still a war happening? Had there been some common ground found? The questions rushed into her head before she could stop them.

"You look a bit pale there, Emilia, are you alright?"

Emilia looked up at Connie and put on a small smile to try and reassure her.

"I'm okay, just a lot to remember, everyone has such silly names that are just ridiculous. Arcane Whispers and Censorship Heroes? Honestly, who comes up with these?" Emilia laughed softly. "Oh, and please, call me Emmy, it feels strange being called Emilia again.

"Okay, Emmy." Connie offered her a soft smile. "I can imagine today was a bit of a mental challenge. How about tomorrow you come with me on a supply run into one of the old cities? Gets you moving and you won't really have to think too much, if anything you'd just be helping me carry things if that sounds alright with you."

Emilia thought it over for a moment before accepting the job. After all, she wanted to earn her keep at Gold Dust Grove, it was the least she could do for them housing and feeding her.

The two of them took a steady ride back to camp, just making it back before sundown. The days were shorter now. Emilia was quiet for the rest of the evening, barely speaking to any of the new friends she had made here. All she could think about was that the people she had come to love down in the pits of hell were all dead. There was nothing left. No matter where she went, a trail of despair appeared to follow close behind. Perhaps she was better off alone.

Seventeen

A supply run was a whole day affair with the cities being quite far away, so after an early morning wake up call from Connie, Emilia prepared herself for the day ahead of her. There was a small group of them heading out today; Connie, Emilia, Myla and Jackson.

Still feeling rather down from the news yesterday, Emilia was still very quiet on the journey there, barely listening to whatever the others were talking about, it was all just background noise to her.

It was almost like an out of body experience, physically she was there, though her mind was elsewhere. Her mind took her back home, back to Rosewood Creek, where she belonged, with Taylor and her family. If she closed her eyes hard enough she could picture herself there now.

The time dragged but eventually the city began to creep into view. Tall, decrepit buildings that may have once stood proud, now diminished to ruins set the scene, the grandeur of them increasing as they grew closer. Emilia had never seen buildings so big. How would one even construct something on this scale? She wondered to herself.

Before diving into the treasures unknown, Connie had suggested they stop for lunch first. It was a unanimous agreement and they all dismounted and sat to eat the sandwiches that they had brought along with them.

Emilia once again heard the chit chat, but was not truthfully paying attention to anything that was really going on - Connie had said this would be more physical than mental, and Emilia was holding her to it.

They decided to split off in pairs to more efficiently cover ground and meet back just before the sun starts to set. Myla and Jackson headed off in one direction and Connie started to lead Emilia in the other.

"So, we're looking for anything that may be of use to us. Any canned goods or rations, medicinal supplies, oh, metal is always a good find but it's definitely getting more rare. Just things that may come in handy, okay?" Connie briefed Emilia, who nodded along unenthusiastically.

The next few hours consisted of silent searches, which Emilia was very thankful for. It was plain to see that Emilia wasn't up for very much in terms of conversation. Slowly, bags started to fill up with a variety of different items and consistently grew heavier the longer they were out.

Emilia was grateful for Connie bringing her along, it was actually doing a very good job of mentally distracting her from her thoughts and slowly, she came back to the present, her head coming down from the clouds she had found herself lost in the past twenty four hours.

Emilia was still struggling with the shock of what she saw yesterday. It had only been destroyed four days ago, she remembered Connie telling her. Four days ago was when she somehow managed to break free of that prison.

Her stomach churned at the thought, but if she had stayed down there any longer she would have perished alongside everyone else. She tried to push the thoughts to the very back of her head, even Emilia wouldn't have survived that.

"Emmy, there's something I think you should see." Came Connie's voice, her tone apprehensive. It was the first words spoken in a while, and Emilia had no verbal response, she just joined Connie's side to see something that surprised her.

There before them, on the wall of the building, was a wanted poster. It wouldn't have been so much of a shock if it was someone they didn't know, but it was plain and clear there in black and white ink - someone was after Emilia.

There was an illustration of her face, accompanied with a description underneath. All she wanted was her peaceful life back, she longed to return to Rosewood Creek, but she had no idea where she was, other than that she was somewhere in Aglotar.

Connie cautiously took the poster from the wall, it appeared to be still quite new, the paper was still very crisp, not aged in the slightest. Emilia watched her eyes shift as she read over the body of the text.

"You know I told you about the rebel group that branded themselves as heroes?" She asked, her eyes leaving the paper and meeting Emilia's. "Turns out that's who is after you. It says here that your dangerous, to not engage with you at any cost and to report you to the nearest 'Afterward Outpost'."

Emilia instinctively took a step back, ready to bolt if need be. She watched as Connie turned the paper over in her hands, revealing a map of local outposts.

"We'll have to make note of these when we return back to camp, they've given us so much free intel." Connie thought aloud, before folding the paper in half, and then again and placing it into her bag. "If we find anymore we'll destroy them, we only need the one copy."

Emilia's entire body was tense, and she watched Connie closely, who gave her a confused look.

"Wait, you don't actually think I'm going to turn you in, do you? After everything you've done for us?" She laughed softly, "Emmy, you're one of us, you are a part of our strange little family. Last time I checked, families looked out for one another, not the opposite. Don't worry, unless you want to, you're not going anywhere."

Emilia still felt stressed, but she felt a wave of clarity wash over her, easing her mind a little, and tears had started to form in the crinkles of her eyes, which she blinked back.

"Thank you, Connie, I can't tell you how much of a relief that is." Was all Emilia was able to choke out, trying not to let her emotions get the better of her. Slowly, the walls she had build up around her were starting to crumble.

It wasn't too long until they met back with Jackson and Myla, who hesitated briefly before producing a handful of posters that they had also come across. Turns out, they enjoyed Emilia's company too, and didn't want people looking for her either, which really did bring her to tears.

Once she had managed to calm herself, and further reassurance from the group, they prepared for the long journey home.

Eighteen

Life at Gold Dust Grove was reminiscent of her life back at Rosewood Creek. They all banded together to make things work. Emilia brought her own set of skills to the group, with knowledge on things from hunting and trapping to baking and sewing.

As previously discussed, Connie had used the map on the poster to locate the outposts and mark them on the big map in the main tent. It had been discussed amongst the people that Emilia belonged here, and that no one would turn her in.

It eased her mind and made Gold Dust Grove truly feel like a home, one she had longed for for the better part of a year.

Emilia became very close with everyone there, she taught Winnie and Jamie helpful survival skills alongside the others and really found her place here.

Time started to fly by here, and before she knew it she had been there for almost a year.

Emilia was closest with Connie, and when she wasn't needed elsewhere she often found herself by her side. Whether it be foraging, planning resource runs, tracking movements from other camps or just simply being with her. She just really enjoyed Connie's company.

She was happier now, too. She found herself laughing more than she had done in quite some time. Life was nice here and she was content. Perhaps though, she had become quite complacent and was slacking in terms of combat training.

Emilia had become so used to the routine at the Whispers' Facility that it felt strange not having to train for hours upon hours each day. It just wasn't really needed here, nor were her powers. She was more than happy to lay low, though. The less attention she received the better really. Though she did indulge in sparring with the others every now and again, after all they all needed to be prepared for anything.

Emilia had learned that the war wasn't over, not technically, but it was no longer as active as it used to be, and Emilia found that it was seldom on her mind. There were no more ongoing attacks, at least none that they knew of. Every now and again, Connie received word from Jep, though Emilia had still yet to meet him, she was glad that he appeared to be alive and still relaying information back to the camp.

Letters from Jep often brought back news of faraway lands, sometimes good and sometimes bad. He informed them of new outpost locations, and where facilities had been destroyed. One letter contacted the location of the largest outpost he had seen - in one of the biggest cities in Aglotar, taking up not just one of the modern buildings that reached upwards towards the sky, but a great expanse of them - they were growing their empire. An empire that Connie still didn't trust to be good.

They discovered less and less wanted posters each time they looted a new city, and Emilia could only hope that they assumed her to be dead. She was getting used to her peaceful life and she was loving it.

She trusted Connie and the others with her life, and had done for quite some time now. Emilia believed that she had also earned the trust of them in return. When they were on longer journeys that took days rather than hours, Emilia could take a watch by herself and no one would feel unsafe, nor would they struggle to sleep.

Though it wasn't often she would take a watch alone, she would often be joined by Connie, who would sit with her, sometimes they would quietly talk, telling tales from their respective pasts. Other times they would do nothing but sit and stare at the stars together, and Emilia would admire the way Connie shone in the light of the moon.

It was approaching a year since Emilia had joined the group, and they were on route to a large city. It was part reconnaissance and part supply run. It was just Connie and Emilia, since this mission was a few days ride away from Gold Dust Grove, they figured the best thing to do was to go with minimal people, so that the camp still had some strong members to protect the others.

It was well into the night when the city came in to view of the two of them, and they decided to lay low in an abandoned building just on the outskirts for the night, and start searching the city at first light. In order to keep undetected, the two of them avoided lighting a fire and just ate cold rations for their evening meal.

The night was cold, but they were sheltered from the wind which helped immensely. Not only that, but they had each other. It wasn't uncommon for them to share a bed for the sake of staying warm. They would do it with the others too, Emilia had no quarrels with cozying up with Myla, Jackson and a few of the others that she had met at Gold Dust Grove when it was needed.

However, sharing a bed with Connie felt different somehow, like there was something more between them. It was unspoken, and nothing had happened between them, but both of them could feel there was something there. They were both just too stubborn to admit it.

The light from the early morning sun started to creep in from the cracks in the walls. Emilia could feel its warmth through the gaps in the boarded up windows, and she was first to awake. Connie looked ever so peaceful in her deep slumber, that she almost didn't want to wake her. Gently, she rocked her shoulders.

"Wakey wakey sleepyhead." She teased softly, "We have lots of work to do."

Naturally, there were grumbles from Connie but she arose slowly, reluctantly. Together they had some cold breakfast before making a plan of action for the day.

They agreed that in order to cover the most ground, one of them would go in one direction of the city, and the other in the opposite direction. It would mean separating, but neither of them wanted to be here for longer than a day, which would hopefully be plenty of time to gather enough resources. At sundown, they would both meet back here for another night and begin the journey home the morning after.

It was a foolproof plan, so long as nothing went wrong.

* * *

The majority of the day was spent filtering into buildings, scouting out any supplies that may come in handy back at camp, searching for any information on the outposts or facility locations, and leaving without a trace.

It was repetitive, but the time passed quite quickly and reminded Emilia not to stay in any one place for too long. She stopped mid afternoon to eat and take a drink, taking the time to ensure Onyx was well and happy, too. Emilia had learned that the mare was very intelligent, and independent too.

Onyx very rarely needed intervention from others and looked after herself for the most part. She had proved herself to be a loyal companion on numerous occasions now. Emilia often felt a twinge of sadness, feeling as though Onyx had left her herd for her, but she had never shown an eagerness to leave Emilia, which she appreciated.

They made a good team together, and often appeared to be on the same wavelength when it came to making decisions. It happened often where Emilia was starting to get the feeling that she needed to leave, only to have Onyx becoming restless moments later, as though she felt the same.

Emilia was busy searching through what appeared to be an old coffee shop. There wasn't much in terms of information here, but there were a few bags of coffee beans that was sure to go down a treat back at the camp. She placed the beans into her bag, along with some metal cutlery that she had found, she was sure Myla would be able to make use of the steel.

Though she wasn't there for too long, Emilia developed an eerie feeling that she was being watched. She turned around to scan her surroundings, but saw nothing suspicious. She noticed that the sun was getting really low now, and that she wouldn't be able to do much more today.

Thankfully, Emilia had been quite successful with her finds, and decided that what she had was likely enough for today. Maybe they would be able to stretch out the supply run to one more day to try and cover more of the city, it was possibly one of the biggest ones they had done so far and there was still a lot of ground to cover.

As she left the building, she was a little surprised to see that Onyx was no where to be seen. Though it wasn't completely unusual for the mare to go for a wander by herself, so she tried not to dwell and slowly started to make her way back to where she started. Emilia instinctively slipped into the shadows between two buildings upon hearing the static of a radio.

"We have a few different groups across the city, target has been sighted here and intel says she is still inside the city, report back if target is sighted or acquired. We have eyes above that you need to report any changes to. Over."

"Copy that, sir. Over."

Emilia knew that voice. Though it was much colder now than the last time she heard it. The kindness behind it was gone, in it's place was nothing. There was no emotion behind those words but she knew exactly who it was before she even saw his face. She started to question her sanity, though, because surely it couldn't be... Could it?

She knew she had to find another way back out of the city - this must have been why Onyx wasn't waiting for her where Emilia had left her. She was too smart to lead them straight to her.

Emilia's heart was pounding, it felt as though it was in her throat. The intensity was almost too much to bare as she wound up at the other end of the alleyway. She stuck to the shadows, trying her best to work her way out of the maze of buildings she found herself lost in.

Up ahead, she saw a smaller group of people in armoured vests, equipped with guns similar to the ones she encountered when she first met Connie, Winnie and Myla. These must be the people that were after her, but what for? To capture her? Do tests on her like they did back at the Whispers' Facility.

Emilia didn't know their intentions just yet, so she wasn't out for blood. She wasn't a killer, nor had she ever been, but she also wanted to get out of here alive.

Silently, she crept up to one of the soldiers - that's all she could assume they were at this point - one that was all by themself. They were looking away from Emilia, which gave her the opportunity to knock them out cold, quickly and quietly.

Emilia disarmed the weapon that they were holding, just in case they woke up sooner than she expected.

She also debated taking the radio, but decided against it as she didn't want it to give her position away.

She crept away into the shadows of another building, but just over half way there she heard a voice on a distant radio and suddenly there was a light on her, she had been spotted.

"Target acquired! Freeze!"

Emilia raised her arms slowly, assessing how many of them she would have to take on. There was four of them left here, it could be an easy fight if she really tried, but it had been quite some time since she last had an encounter like this.

A sly smile spread across her face, the adrenaline rushing through her body made the decision for her.

"No."

Emilia jumped right into the action, throwing a sphere of blue light towards them. Surely, they didn't expect her to just stand there and take it, they must have known she would fight back, and she watched as it collided with the one the soldiers and knocked them back a few feet.

Guns started to fire at her and she dodged all bullets with ease, she was well and rested and at full strength, a cocky smile stretching across her face as she realised she was stronger than she thought without constant practice.

She threw more balls of light at them, knocking them back one by one. She didn't really want to cause harm or be violent, she was just trying to get them back enough to give her chance to escape. She felt someone else watching her, though and when she had a spare second she whipped her head around to see a figure standing atop one of the buildings.

Emilia saw he had a bow, with a quiver full of arrows. He hadn't drawn one yet, he was just watching her from a distance. He wasn't an issue. Not just yet, anyways. She doubted that one of those arrows would reach her from the distance anyways, though she didn't want to underestimate him as a threat.

One final wave of power took the others out. Not killing them, just knocking them out. Emilia checked for a pulse, just to be sure. Satisfied, she took a gun for herself, placing it in to the holder than she attached to her waist, before walking off, back to the shadows from where she felt safest. Keeping on edge as she didn't know what could be around the next corner.

"She's more powerful than we thought, she's just taken out four of our men with the wave of her hand. Be vigilant, she's headed your way. I'm following behind, we need to catch her off guard I think. Sending more guys your way. Over."

Emilia couldn't help but smirk at the radio transmission, they did not have the element of surprise on their side. She did, and she was armed and ready for a fight. A part of her had missed this, though she would never admit it out loud. Unfortunately, the Whispers' had taught her how to be a soldier, a fighter, and as much as she hated it even Emilia had to admit it was coming in handy.

Adrenaline was flowing through her veins, she was worried for Connie, but these guys weren't after Connie, they were after her. This gave her a slight peace of mind, not only was she causing a distraction and drawing them all to her, but Connie was talented herself, she had been training with Emilia and so she knew first hand that she could hold her own in a fight.

She stretched her arms out and took hold of her dagger, instinct told her that this was about to get a little more difficult.

Emilia emerged from the shadows, all eyes turned to her as she made her way through the soldiers that got in her way. One on one combat was more fun when it was serious. She threw punches with strength she didn't know she had, using her dagger when needed to cause additional damage.

She had the upper hand in almost every aspect and it didn't appear that many of them had powers like she did. She came across a couple of people who seemed to have greater strength, or were quicker than her, but she was always stronger, faster, more ready for a fight.

That was until she came face to face with the one person she didn't want to see. She was right about the voice from earlier.

Bailey stood between Emilia and her freedom, she had taken on everyone else and won. She sheathed her dagger and lowered her arms. As she did so, she noticed movement above her out of the corner of her eyes. The archer was back, and he was closer this time.

Bailey looked confused as to why she put away her weapons, leaving herself defenceless. He kept a hold on his own gun, ready for action.

"I still won't fight you, Bailey. They couldn't make me before, they won't make me now." Emilia said smoothly, with a confidence she didn't realise she had. She had believed him to be dead for over a year. She had already grieved him, along with the other friends she had made in the Whisper's facility. She was again met with nothing but confusion.

"How do you know my name?" He asked skeptically. That hurt. They had made him forget her. Forget the time they shared together. It hurt, and she was mad. A hand instinctively reached towards her dagger, but she was determined not to fight him, not after everything that happened between them.

"I refuse to fight you, so I am so sorry." She said quieter than before. She had been actively listening to any movements from above her, and though she was starting to let her emotions get the better of her, she remained calm, sensing the archers intentions and actions. She felt the way the arrow moved the second it was let loose. The arrow intended for her. It moved quickly through the air, but Emilia calmly moved to the side. "I'm sorry, Bailey."

The arrow went straight into his upper thigh, causing him to drop down to the ground in pain. Emilia didn't want to stick around, so she started to walk away, making notes of his reaction. The arrow must have contained something to tranquillise her, as she saw Bailey loose consciousness pretty soon after he was struck.

She picked up the pace as she wove her way through the darkness, trying to figure out where she was in the city and how to escape it.

Eventually, she was forced to stop as she reached a dead end, and a smooth wall that was too high to just climb over. Emilia turned around to go back, but as she did so three soldiers rounded the corner, leaving her trapped.

Guns were raised and aimed towards her, whilst the one in the middle radioed their position across to the others for them to come and get her.

Emilia was tired of fighting, and a little disoriented after seeing Bailey again, it was almost like seeing a ghost. A ghost who had no memory of her at all.

"Okay, you've got me trapped between guns and a wall, clearly you have the upper hand. Yet you haven't shot me on sight, which means you need me for something." She talked at them, they gave each other a knowing look that proved she was at least a little bit right in her assumption. As she spoke, she started to look around her surroundings, trying to figure out a plan.

"Good to know, so it would really be a shame if I escaped. Clearly, that archer of yours is the only one with whatever you're using to put people to sleep, and some of it was just wasted on one of your guys."

Emilia could see that she was rattling their nerves a little from their expressions and awkward glances between one another. It made her smile, just a little.

"Also good to know. It would be such a shame for you guys if I figured out a way to escape whilst I've been distracting you, wouldn't it?" She taunted, leading them to raise their guns again that had slowly been lowering as she spoke.

"Approaching now, just hold her there a little longer! Over!" Came a voice from the radio, she could hear from the laboured speech and heavy breathing that Mr. Archer was racing to get to them, but it was too late.

Emilia kicked the metal bins next to her at the three soldiers, while throwing a light sphere at a fire escape, causing the ladder to fall down to where she could reach it. She laughed as she jumped towards it, grabbing the rungs and pulling herself upwards before racing all the way to the roof, dodging the bullets fired at her from the ground as she moved quickly, but she felt it necessary to wave at the three soldiers as she disappeared from their view, just to taunt them that little bit more.

As she reached the top she met the archer as he jumped from the building next to her on to the one she was on now. He immediately fired an arrow at her, whether it was one that causes paralysis, she didn't know, and she wasn't about to stick around to find out.

She started to sprint the opposite way, ducking, leaping and even rolling away from any arrows fired towards her. It was difficult, but she was leeching from the adrenaline rocking her body and using it to her advantage. She was terrified, but she leapt from one building to another. Pausing for a moment to catch her breath and recover - it was further than she thought and she almost didn't make it!

Emilia had no time to sit around though, and was back up and running for her life. She had a much better view from the city from here and she could see the end. It wasn't the way they came in, but she was happier this way, it meant she was leading them away from Connie. The archer was still hot on her heels, which meant she had to keep moving.

In the distance she saw something move across the ground with haste, it was Onyx. Emilia beamed from ear to ear and whistled to catch her attention. If she timed it right, this could be the perfect getaway.

Ducking away from yet another arrow, she spotted another fire escape and began a swift descent. Hopefully, the way she changed course threw the soldiers off slightly and she saw Onyx approaching the alleyway she was stumbling down in to.

The thuds of her hooves hitting the ground repeatedly grew louder and Emilia leant over the barrier, taking a breath. There wasn't far to go now, but Onyx was moving fast. She had to time it just right. She mentally counted herself down before throwing herself from the metal fire escape.

Emilia had never felt luckier, she landed atop Onyx, who didn't even slow down, not really. After adjusting herself into a proper riding position, she had a small celebration, punching the air with a hand before gripping the reins and preparing to race away into the night.

Just when she thought she was in the clear, Onyx let out a cry of pain and fell down to the ground, taking Emilia with her. Emilia didn't have time to realise what happened before she felt a searing pain take over her skin. She looked about frantically to see the Archer dismount a horse of his own and start to approach her.

"We got her guys," He spoke flatly into the radio. "We're going to need the armoured truck."

The Censorship Agency

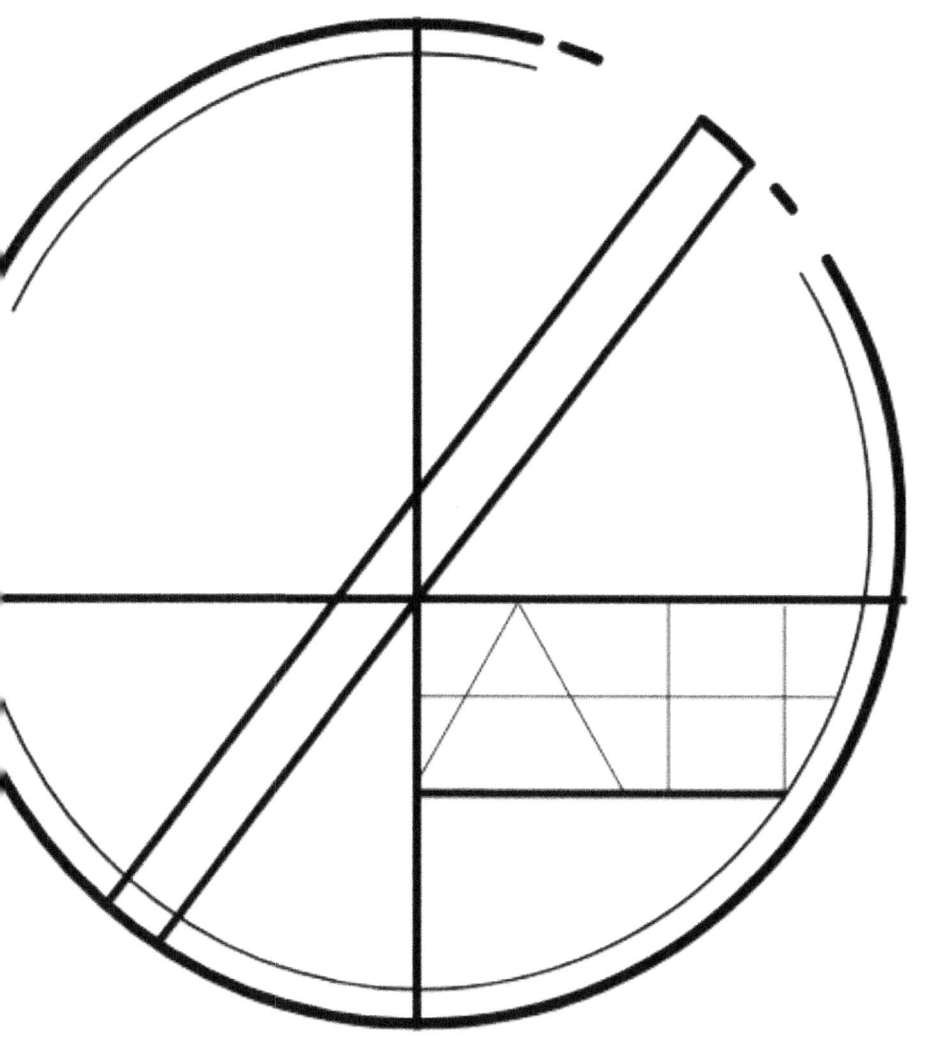

Ebratha

ROSEWOOD CREEK

ROANLOCH

Nineteen

Unable to move or speak, Emilia could only watch as the next events unfolded. A large vehicle pulled up near her, and she was moved into it. Unable to object or fight back, all she could do was let them. She hated every second of this. She would rather be unconscious, knocked out cold.

One of the soldiers approached her with a syringe of some kind of liquid. Taking her right arm and injecting her with whatever it was, she felt powerless in the moment. She could see that the soldier was saying something, but she couldn't hear a thing.

The pain, thankfully, didn't last long, but the numbness that followed was almost as bad. Despite the lack of posters they had seen in quite some time, it turned out the Agency was in fact, still looking for her and she was hopefully going to find out why.

She lost track of how long she was in the truck for, and had no sense of geographical location, either, but something told her that she was being taken to the main outpost, the one Jep had told them about in his letters.

Eventually, the journey came to an end and the engine was silent and still. Emilia was still unable to move a single muscle, so was in fact carried in by two of the soldiers. It was brighter than the Facility she had been in, more natural light too, but then again this place was almost the polar opposite of the underground base she had been kept in. She would be almost up in the clouds with how tall these buildings could get.

They dragged her through, passing a number of rooms until they got to one that looked almost clinical. It was bright with artificial lighting that strained her eyes. They placed her into the corner of the room, and she watched as a shiny, slightly translucent barrier now separated her from the rest of the room.

Emilia wasn't sure how long she had been in there for, but she watched as people took turns being in the room with her - like they were being a personal guard just for her. She couldn't understand it, but slowly, she started to regain the feeling in her limbs.

She had stopped paying attention to how often the soldiers rotated, it wasn't too frequent, but it appeared to be every few hours, like they were taking shifts watching her. She eventually managed to stand on her own two feet and she approached the barrier. She cautiously raised an open palm to it.

There was a slight shock as she made contact with it, but it didn't linger nor continue to shock her. It was firm, though it looked as though there was nothing there, an invisible barrier had her trapped here. Emilia figured there was no point in trying to break it down, at least not yet while she was still a little shaky from whatever they did to her.

Emilia looked across the room, there was a modest control panel, covered with different sized buttons, sliders and even a telephone, next to a small desk, with a chair to sit on, though it didn't look particularly comfortable.

There was a man sat at the desk now, reading a book, he had quite dark skin, along with dark brown hair and deep, chocolate brown eyes to match. He looked quite skinny, but appeared to have quite strong, slightly muscular arms.

It took Emilia a minute or two but she eventually recognised him, he looked different in this light, but it was the archer that managed to take her down last night. Instinctively, she reached to her waistline for her dagger.

"Do you really think they'd just let you keep your weapons on you?" He asked without even looking up from his book, turning a page, disinterested in what she was doing. "They're not the brightest, but they're not completely stupid."

Emilia scowled at him, but he didn't appear to care. She didn't say anything else, she assumed she would find out why she was here in due time, potentially an explanation of sorts. Nothing, he just sat there and read his book until another soldier came to relieve him from duty.

This one, however, was very interested in Emilia. Question after question after question.
Are you with the Whispers?
Where is your current facility located?
What information do you have on the facility that you came from? Was it destroyed and why?
What training do you have?

Emilia just gave them a funny look and retreated further into her corner. They tried to get information from her, but quickly gave up a little when they realised she didn't want to talk. The next few guards were all alike, trying to interrogate her but eventually giving in and just watching her.

She stayed in there for a number of days, sometimes when the guards would change over, a meal would be brought with it, which they used to try and get information from her before giving it to her, but they couldn't just withhold her food so they would eventually cave and just allow her to eat. There was only one of them that said not a word to her.

The archer.

On this particular meal time shift change, the archer was the one to relieve the current soldier of duty. He placed the food into the barrier for her before sitting down at the desk and opening his book.

Emilia cautiously started to eat, smelling the food first to see if there was anything off about it, inspecting it as best she could.

"If they wanted to kill you by now they would have, it's just food, miss." He spoke softer than the others would, and he was more respectful, too. He turned away, returning to the desk where he pulled out his book.

Even though he was eventually the one that took Emilia down, surprisingly, she had a good feeling about him, and she took his word about the food and began to eat. The food was bland, tough and chewy, but she couldn't really complain, at least they were feeding her and it was still somehow better than what she used to have at the Whispers' Facility.

"So," Emilia spoke up after finishing her meal. "Why is it, that everyone else is all up in my personal space trying to figure out my business, yet you just don't seem to care in the slightest?"

"Well, that's simple. I don't care." He said, swiftly diverting his attention back to the book.

Emilia felt surprised by the honestly, and it must have shown in her face, because when he looked back up at her a few seconds later, and shook his head gently.

"I was briefed that we had a mission to take you in under any circumstances, providing that you were alive. That is what I was paid for. I was not informed about babysitting you and playing a hundred and one questions, so I just see this as free time now to have a bit of downtime. Catch up on some reading."

He may not have realised it, but he had given her quite a lot of information to work with there and it intrigued her.

"So, what is it you're reading?"

"Did I or did I not just tell you that I didn't want to play a hundred and one questions?"

"Well, no." Emilia shrugged off his passive aggressive retort. "You said you weren't informed about playing a hundred and one questions. Not that you didn't want to."

She received a look that made her bite down on her bottom lip in an attempt not to laugh.

"Sorry," She said through a smile. "I am just tired of the seriousness everywhere I go. That and I'm so bored in here, there's nothing to do. Look at me, I'm restless!"

Emilia received a small smile in return.

"Will you at least tell me your name?" Emilia asked with a cheeky look in her eyes. The archer pondered it for a moment.

"If I answer that can we spend the rest of our time today in silence?" Reluctantly, Emilia nodded. "Okay, good. My name is Noah."

Emilia opened her mouth to speak, but Noah immediately held up a finger and wagged it at her, a cheeky grin on his own face as he returned to his book again.

"Ah ah ah," Noah taunted. "You promised me silence."

Twenty

Emilia had been in there for about a week, and she had gotten to know the archer fairly well. Noah never seemed to care about getting answers from her for his employer, and the two of them had started talking about their personal lives on occasion.

Emilia had learned that Noah was recruited by the Agency quite some time ago; he was all by himself in the northern mountains for a long time with nowhere else to go after the lost his family during the war. He was a skilled archer - she knew that much already - as he had to learn to hunt to survive out there.

News about Noah's skill with the bow had traveled south and made it's way to the people here, who figured he would be a great asset to their ever growing team.

Emilia had learned a lot about them these past few days, this was their main outpost, which they labeled The Censorship Agency - most just skipped over the middle part though. Their main job was to seek out and rehabilitate anyone that had been taken to The Whispers. They often struggled with the transition back into normal life and needed a little guidance.

Another thing they did was to search and destroy any facilities that they knew about, freeing everyone inside. That was why Bailey was here. They found him being taken back to the Facility after an attempted break out, which is how they found it. They released everyone in there and swiftly destroyed the building, just in case they tried to start again.

    Bailey had been grateful for all their help, and decided to stay with them - to help others. Emilia didn't feel all that surprised, that did sound like something he would do. Unfortunately, he had very little knowledge of his time in there and wasn't able to pass on any information, he had appeared to have suffered some memory loss from whatever had happened to him. He found the work fulfilling, and stayed with the Agency all this time. A whole year after the facility had been destroyed.

    The main reason they had been searching so hard for Emilia was because they believed she was under the influence of The Whispers, and was a danger to society - hence why they were keeping her withheld from their staff.

    Noah had passed along to his superiors that Emilia is not in any way, affiliated with them and that she is not a danger to anyone as she never received the conditioning that so many others had, but he had yet to receive the order to let her go.

    "Wakey wakey, Warren." He spoke cheerfully sliding her breakfast through the forcefield. "I managed to get you the good stuff today!"

Emilia could smell the food before she even opened her eyes, and she was in shock at the sight before her, a hot breakfast! There were some strips of meat, a couple of eggs and some toasted bread with soft butter. It was like a dream! She immediately dived in and savoured every mouthful.

"Not to sound rude, Noah, but you seem in a particularly good mood today, something happen?"

"Nothing's happened, but my fiancé is due back today and I'm just happy she's going to be back. I haven't seen her in like, two months." He said, a grin going from ear to ear across his face.

"Ah," Emilia smiled back. "That certainly explains it. You've never mentioned her before, though, so I had no idea!"

"You never asked." Noah chuckled softly. "I met her because of this place, she's honestly the best thing to happen to me. She is so bubbly and positive and just a ray of sunshine despite everything she's been through. I can't be late to meet her, either, she will pull me up on it."

Emilia couldn't help but laugh softly herself.

"I used to know someone like that, she was my best friend. I haven't seen her since before the bomb went off and ruined everything. Before the Whisper's took me away." She sighed softly, "Sorry, went on a little trip down memory lane there. Does she have any powers like us?"

"She has powers, but not like us." Noah stated. Emilia had learned about his incredible eyesight, which didn't sound all that impressive at first, but she had seen his accuracy firsthand and knew now why he had such an advantage from the rooftops.

"She has this way of manipulating emotions that I haven't seen before, it's kind of scary how fast she can change a person. She's just starting to learn how to revive memories too, not just hers but she can bring memories back to people. I think they're going to try and do it on your friend, Bailey, once she's back. See if he can restore any of his memories."

It was interesting, and Emilia was hanging on to every word. She thought back to the day she realised she was no longer in the Facility and how she had no memory of escaping.

"If she has time, I have a memory I would like to try and find, too. It's from the night I escaped the Whispers'. To this day, I have no idea what happened."

Their chat was interrupted by the ringing of a telephone in the room. Noah immediately turned to answer it. Emilia couldn't hear what was being said, just a few mumbles from Noah.

Eventually, he placed the receiver back down and turned towards Emilia with a smile.
"They would really appreciate it if you stayed just a little longer," Emilia rolled her eyes at the statement, they hadn't exactly given her any chances to leave.

"But they understand if you wish to leave. If you are happy to stay a little longer, they have a room for you, with clean clothes and a soft bed."

The shock was apparent on her face as she tried to comprehend his words.

"They're happy to let me go?"

"If you want to leave, yes. They will let you go."

Emilia stood up, ready to jump at the chance, but hesitated for a moment. Would she be able to cope without knowing what happened? When there was someone here who might be able to help her find out? Would she ever get another chance at this? Staying just a little bit longer wouldn't be such a bad thing, right?

* * *

Noah escorted Emilia up towards the living quarters, they were up a couple of stories. All the rooms were the same, and you were able to fit eight rooms per floor it seemed, four on either side. Some people opted to live outside of the city, or in a different building close to this one, so it wasn't overcrowded here at least, despite how many people seemed to work for the agency.

Eventually, they reached the one that would be hers, at least for now. Emilia looked inside, it wasn't anything spectacular, but there was a nice sized bed, a small desk and dresser, and taking up a corner was another room, which she found to be a private bathroom. Again, nothing special, just a toilet, sink and shower, but it was all hers, at least for now.

"I'll leave you to get settled and changed, they'll be serving lunch soon downstairs if you want to join, I'll wait in there for you if you like."

"Yeah, that would be nice, thank you, Noah. This place seems really big, would you mind maybe showing me around a bit after lunch?"

Noah nodded in agreement, and said a quick goodbye, leaving Emilia all by herself. She peered out of the window at the city. The sun was high in the sky, shining light across the tall buildings. She could appreciate the beauty for what it was, but it couldn't hold a candle to Gold Dust Grove. She missed it, and wanted to return as soon as she could, but she just couldn't pass up an opportunity like this. To finally know what happened that day.

After a nice, hot shower, she changed into the clothes that had been left in the dresser. It wasn't anything glamorous, just a plain black, long sleeved top, and some tan cargo bottoms. They were comfortable, and fit quite nicely, actually. They were loose around her legs, but the elasticated waist ensured that they wouldn't be going anywhere. Out of habit, she pulled the drawstrings into a tight knot, just to be sure.

Atop the dresser there was a brush and some hair ties that had been left for her, too. Taking a deep breath, Emilia got to work and managed to tame her hair into two braids, securing them at the ends. She was satisfied and felt a little more human now.

Emilia kept walking down until she reached a different layout - this one was much more open, and busy too. After a few seconds she could smell food and knew that this must be the lunch hall that Noah had told her about, but she couldn't see him.

Nervously, she headed up to where she saw other people getting lunch from and joined the line. It wasn't long till she got to the front. She opted for some sort of stew, with mashed potatoes on the side. It smelled fantastic, and she couldn't wait to dig in.

She didn't mind sitting alone, in fact right now she preferred it. There were only two people she knew at this agency: one wasn't in here and the other one didn't remember who she was, and she wasn't ready for that conversation just yet.

"Sorry, sorry I'm late, Tay got here sooner than expected!" She heard Noah apologise from behind her. She lifted her head to tell him it was okay, but she was lost for words. Emilia knew that freckled face, framed with wavy locks of auburn hair. It was a face she never thought she would see again.

"Taylor?"

"Emmy?"

"I thought you were dead!" Emilia could feel the tears threatening to spill. "Oh my god, you're alive. You're alive!"

Emilia had stood from the table the second she saw Taylor's face, pulling her into a tight embrace. She stayed there for some time. A range of emotions cycled their way through Emilia, taking her through the motions. As far as she was aware, Taylor was now the only family she had left. Slowly, she found the strength to release the younger girl, her hands shaking.

Emilia wasn't the only one with strong emotions. Taylor had streaks of tears down her cheeks, her face damp.

"I can't believe it's really you." Taylor managed to choke out between quiet sobs. "I'm so happy to see you, Emilia. I really am. I thought the girl on the posters looked familiar, but I didn't think anyone else survived the blast. I thought everyone else was dead."

There was a deep sadness in her voice. Taylor had survived, but at what cost? To see everyone she loved die? The town she grew up in burn to the ground? Emilia had no clue what her little town looked like right now, but she could only assume it was in ruins. The thought broke her heart.

Something clicked for both of them at the same time; they realised that each of them now had powers, at least based on what Noah had told her.

There was a childlike excitement that Emilia hadn't felt in years, and she hadn't realised how much she had missed that feeling. Noah took a backseat as the two girls started to catch up on years of separation.

Emilia gasped loudly, placing a hand over her open mouth in an attempt to stifle it as she realised something else.

"You are engaged?!" She looked between the two of them, Taylor started to nod enthusiastically. The thought took Emilia by surprise, her best friend wasn't the young girl that she used to be. Both of them had grown up substantially over the last few years.

Taylor raised her hand up, and something caught Emilia's eye. A beautiful silver ring, with detailed engraving that made it look like the branch of a tree, with a stunning emerald gemstone in the middle. It was small, but Emilia was taken aback by the beauty of it.

"I am. I met Noah when the agency came to recruit me. They came to Rosewood Creek, to see if there were any survivors. All they found was me. They promised me safety, shelter and food, which is more than I had there, so I took a chance and went with them. Noah and me, we hit it off immediately. I can't imagine how I would have managed without him"

The smile on both their faces said it all, they were young and very much in love, and nothing could possibly come between them. In that moment, all

Emilia could think about was Connie. It had been over a week, at the very least, would they be worried for her? Searching, maybe?

"I'm very happy for you. For both of you, really." Emilia's smile was fading. "I don't want to rush you, but I really can't stay much longer. I want to, but I have people that need me. People that I need to see." Taylor nodded in understanding.

"Noah has already asked me about helping you recover your memories from that night." She started, speaking almost as though she was trying to choose her words carefully. "Given that you both came from the same place, and the events were roughly around the same time, I think it would be best to try and get your memories, and Mr Larson's memory back at the same time."

Emilia was hesitant, she had willingly let Bailey be shot by one of Noah's arrows, granted, it was aimed for her but she was able to move out of the way before it struck. Taylor could see how she reacted, and jumped in again to try and put her mind at ease.

"I promise, it's in both of your best interests. If it makes you feel better, it will be in a controlled environment too, so nothing will happen to either of you while you're there."

Taylor's reassuring voice eased any nerves that Emilia had, and she agreed.

Twenty One

Emilia took a deep breath to calm herself as she looked in the mirror. Taylor and herself had spent the rest of the previous day catching up, swapping tales and joking around. By the time Emilia made it up to bed, she was so tired that she passed out the second her head hit the pillow.

The appeal of working for the agency was as clear as day, you received a very comfortable place to lay your head at night, with your own private bathroom, hot meals served throughout the day and plenty of tasks to keep you going and give you purpose in life.

It was almost time to regain her memories, hopefully. Emilia had spent the morning on the gymnasium level, working out some of her anxieties.

Now, she was fresh and refreshed after a nice hot shower, and was counting down the minutes until she had to go down and meet Taylor and Bailey in one of the office-like rooms.

Emilia was nervous, but the sooner she did this, the sooner she would be able to return to Gold Dust Grove, back to the life she was just starting to settle into.

Bailey was already in the room, ready and waiting, like he was ready to get this over with just as much as

Emilia was. Taylor was just outside the door, waiting for Emilia with a soft, reassuring smile.

"Are you ready?" She asked Emilia, who simply nodded and followed her lead into the room. It was a peculiar set up, the desk that was in here had been pushed up against the wall to clear some floor space. There were large cushions on the floor, all in a single line.

Taylor took the middle seat, crossing her legs and getting herself comfy. Bailey also sat down, Emilia quickly followed suit. Taylor outstretched one hand to Bailey and one to Emilia.

"Hold on to me as long as you can. I don't know what we're about to witness and it may be difficult." Her voice was gentle, addressing both of them. "As long as you are physically connected to me, I can keep a hold of the memory, but once you let go, it fades. I need you both to think back, to the very last point that you can remember before the missing memories, because that will be where we start, okay?"

Taylor checked in with both of them to ensure they both understood, and once satisfied she took a deep breath herself and closed her eyes, letting Emilia and Bailey both get themselves comfortable and ready.

Emilia watched as Bailey looked over at her, deep down he must know who she was, or at the very least recognise her. They spent a whole year together, prisoners of the same organisation. She had missed him, but the man sitting across from her was nothing but a shell of who he used to be.

Taking Taylor's hand in her own, Emilia closed her eyes and took a shaky breath, doing as she was told and trying her best to think back to that day. She didn't really want to relive it, but she needed to know what happened, for her own sanity.

Emilia opened her eyes and she was back at The Whispers' Facility, the last day she remembered being here. She had no control over her actions or her body; all she could do was watch as the events unfolded before her. This was the part she did not want to relive, but at least she couldn't feel the pain of Bailey's punches this time around.

It was truly horrific, but eventually they got to the end of the fight, where Emilia tried her hardest to get through to Bailey before she started to lose her consciousness. Emilia thought she too was going to fade and that the memory would go with it, but she didn't. She was able to see what happened after she fell to the floor.

Bailey took a few steps back, away from Emilia, watching in shock as he seemed to regain control of his actions. A look of pure rage and hatred crossed his face, and he threw the scimitar up towards the spectators, the ones watching him, writing notes on him. Making sure he was being a good puppet. It went straight into one of them, and shrieks of pain filled the room. The others started to yell, the bell ringing out again, they were trying to regain control of Bailey, but it was no use. They kept ringing the alarm again to see if that forced him back into the submission of the conditioning.

Bang.

It was all Bailey, he took his fists to the wall, and with strength even he didn't know he had he somehow burst through the solid walls, and behind it was a fire escape. He had taken another sword and sealed the doors to the arena with it, buying them some time, hopefully.

Bailey picked up the dagger Emilia had been using to defend herself, attaching it to his belt before scooping Emilia up into his arms, as gently as he could. He carried her out of that arena, up the seemingly endless flights of stairs of the fire escape, and he burst through the door at the top.

It was the middle of the night, it was dark. Bailey just ran. As fast as he could while carrying Emilia, any wounds he had from her didn't matter right now. He was filled with anger, guilt and sadness and he couldn't handle it.

After so long, Bailey carefully laid Emilia's unconscious body on the ground. "I'm sorry, I am so so sorry. This is going to hurt when you wake up." He spoke softly, pulling the dagger out. Hands were shaking, and he hesitated, but he knew what he had to do. He cut into Emilia's arm, removing the tracking chip inside that they had put in the day she got there.

Thinking quickly, he ripped at the fabric of Emilia's shirt, tying it around the open wound to help stop the bleeding as best he could. Bailey stomped on the tracking chip multiple times, just to be sure that it was completely destroyed, before throwing it as far as he could.

Putting the dagger away again, he picked Emilia back up, just praying she wasn't dead. Bailey kept pushing, trying to get her as far away from the Facility as he could. The night sky was slowly getting lighter, and he knew that the sun would be rising soon, which meant they would be able to find them easier.

Bailey found a small clearing by a river, Emilia started to recognise the land around her, and he did everything he could to ensure that Emilia's body was hidden - placing her in the tall grass, almost at the tree line and scattering some of the crisp autumn leaves atop her helpless body in an attempt to cover her up . He was sobbing by this point, he didn't want to leave her, but he also wanted to try and lure them away from her as best her could. He placed a soft kiss on her forehead.

"I love you. Stay alive."

The words were heartfelt, and Emilia could feel their meaning, even if this was nothing more than a memory from her unconscious state of mind. Then that was it, he was gone.

Emilia was left there for quite some time, in which she assumed Bailey's memories were still going from the rest of that evening. She was left alone with her unconscious body and her thoughts until it all started to fade away.

Emilia slowly opened her eyes, readjusting to the brightness of the room. The lights had been dimmed on this occasion, but they were still quite harsh. Not a word was said between them, the silence deafening and unbearable.

It had only been a few moments, though it felt like a lot longer. Bailey eyes met Taylors. "Thank you." He said, voice quiet and low. He stood up, and without another word he left the room.

Emilia's hands were kept loosely on her lap, as she thought it all through. For the first time in her life, she felt her heart torn two ways, and she didn't know what to do. A part of her wished that she had taken the first chance to run, get as far away from this place as she could and make her way back to Gold Dust Grove.

However, if she had done that, she wouldn't have been reunited with Taylor. She would have never learned about how Bailey had been the one to set her free of that hell. The one that gave her another shot at life.

"Take your time," Came Taylor's soft voice, it was quiet; delicate. "I can imagine that was a lot to process. Do you need a minute alone?" She offered gently.

Emilia shook her head slowly, the last thing she needed right now, was to be alone. Taylor understood, and scooted herself over to be closer to Emilia, letting her lean on her for support.

"I don't know what to do."

Emilia said, her voice weak. It was the first time in a long time she was allowing herself to be truly vulnerable. She had built walls up around herself for everyone else, not knowing who to trust. Taylor was the only one that Emilia knew she could be safe around, the only person she truly trusted.

Taylor didn't say anything else, she just stayed with her whilst Emilia came to grips with what she had seen, an arm wrapped around her, providing comfort and support.

Twenty Two

The rest of the day was a forgettable blur, and Emilia had spent most of it in her room, processing and thinking everything over.

Staring at the city from the window, she looked further, past the tall, incredible buildings. Maybe somewhere out there she could find a place to call home again, maybe even find Rosewood Creek.

Perhaps Taylor would come with her, of course she could bring Noah along, too. Maybe Connie would be willing to make the journey to her hometown. Sadly, she didn't know the way, and she remembered Meladia's words, that she would only know the way home when the time came.

Frustrated, she pushed open the window, climbing out onto the fire escape. She wandered up to the very top of the building, hoping she would find some sort of clarity up there.

There was nothing to be found but the brisk, late autumn wind. Winter would be coming before she knew it, and all she knew that she didn't want to be alone during that time. The winter was harsh, and without company she would surely freeze to a bitter end. She had to make a decision soon.

Unaware of how long she had been up there, she watched as the sun started to set, the sky was radiant and full of colour. The cold night air was setting in, and with each exhale, she could physically see how cold it was.

"I had a feeling you might be up here." A low voice came from behind her. It took her by surprise, but she didn't have it in her to even flinch, let alone turn around. "Everyone has been looking for you, they thought you'd just up and left."

"Would it even matter if I did?" Emilia said in a tired voice, slowly looking over at Bailey. "What do they even need me for, anyways? Can I not just go if I wanted to?"

"Well, I suppose you could, but they were hoping for a bit of cooperation in helping with their missions." Bailey shrugged, trying not to let her negativity influence him. "It's really not that bad here, anyways. Hot food, shelter, something to strive towards."

"I really don't need anyone else to try and sell me this place." She said flatly. "I just want to go home. Leave everything behind and go back to my old life, on my farm, in my little town."

"I'm sorry, Emmy."

"My name is Emilia." She was blunt, and it was harsh, so she tried to right herself. "Sorry, I just can't do this right now."

Emilia stood up and walked towards the edge of the building, trying to give herself a bit more space. Although earlier she couldn't fathom being alone, right now she felt as though she needed it. She heard Bailey muttering behind her, and radio fuzz following.

"Hey, hey, it's alright, just... Can you just come away from the edge?" He pleaded, and Emilia hadn't even realised how things had looked. She laughed wryly, but obliged and took a couple of steps backwards, sitting down again and looking out onto the horizon.

"I wasn't... I wasn't going to do anything." She tried to reassure him. "Even if I did, I don't think it would have mattered. I don't think I could die even if I did want to. I'm a part of something bigger than all of this, apparently, but I just don't know what she meant."

Bailey frowned, as though trying to understand what she was telling him, and sat near her. Not directly beside her, he didn't want to be too forward.

"Don't know what who meant?"

"She's called Meladia, she gifted me these powers, told me I'm a protector and to use them for good. She said that there was something coming that was more dangerous than anything in our realm, but I haven't heard anything since the Facility. It's been a year, and nothing seems to have changed, and I just don't know what she meant."

Bailey appeared to have lost some of the colour from his face.

"Who else knows?" He asked, clearly showing signs of stress, fear, tension. "Have you told anyone else about this?"

"Bailey, what do you know?" Emilia asked, her own worry growing.

"Not much, there have been some rumours though. Rumours that The Whispers' have found, or made a gate to another world, one that they're trying to find out how to open. From what I've heard, they haven't succeeded, at least not yet. Come to think of it, I briefly remember someone saying that it had a glow around it - at least from what their sources said."
"A glow?"

"Mhmm. A silvery blue glow." Bailey looked at Emilia with a knowing look. "I think that's why the agency have been looking for you for over a year. Maybe you're the key to open it." It was like everything was slowly slotting in to place in both of their minds. "They've been trying to make sure that the Whispers' didn't find you first, I think I finally understand why."

"Do you trust them, though?" Emilia spoke softly, suddenly feeling as though she wasn't as safe as she first hoped. This was her Bailey, though. The memories that Taylor had revived had also brought him back. This was the man she shared a life with for the year they were trapped.

"I think so, they've done so much for me."
Emilia shook her head.

"That's not enough. I need you to be completely sure you trust them, or I can't."

Bailey looked hesitant, like he maybe wasn't so sure himself.

"They keep a lot of things confidential, things only certain people know about."

Emilia briskly made her way back to the fire escape, decision made.

"Where are you going?" Bailey called after her.

"Away from here, you coming or not?"

"Lock down the building, we need to make sure she doesn't get away."

Bailey's radio came to life again and the two of them shared a look as they started to make their way down the fire escape. Emilia's heart was racing.

"What about Taylor and Noah?" Emilia stopped in her tracks. "I can't just leave them. They must know by now that I'm close with them, what if they try to use that against us?"

"We'll get them out, but we're going to have to be quick if they're starting to lock down the building." Bailey stated, without a second thought about it. The confidence in his words filled Emilia with certainty and together they started to come up with a plan as they made their way down.

"*They're not on the roof, they must have made a run for it.*" Came a different voice from the radio. "*Heading back down to level three, over.*"

"*Don't go. It's a trap.*" Came a different voice. One they both recognised. "*I've tuned into your frequency only, do not respond. I repeat, do not respond.*" Noah's voice crackled through over the other voice. "*They've taken Taylor. Meet me on level seven.*"

Bailey was hesitant, but Emilia trusted Noah and insisted they meet him, so he lead the way. They opened the window as quietly as they could and peered inside, they couldn't see anyone as first, but Noah emerged from the shadows he was hidden in.

"I'm glad you got here okay." Noah greeted them, "Taylor is a part of the trap down on level three, they're trying to draw you in, but I don't know why. A couple of days ago they were happy to just let you go, but now they're doing everything in their power to make sure you can't leave,"

"I'll explain later, right now, we need to get Taylor and get as far away from here as we can. I promise I'll tell you everything as soon as I can." Emilia's words were frantic, but she knew Noah most likely just wanted Taylor safe, just as she did. He reached to his side briefly, before holding something out towards Emilia.

A grin spread across her face as her dagger was returned to her.

"Oh we are going to have some fun, aren't we?" She looked between them. Noah also had a variety of weapons for Bailey to choose from.

Armed and ready, they quickly formed a plan; Emilia was to be a distraction. She would go down to level three and hopefully all eyes would be on her, giving Bailey and Noah chance to free Taylor.

Phase two was to steal horses from their stables, they wouldn't get far enough away on foot so the best bet was to use what they had to their advantage and it was more than likely that any vehicles they had would have tracking devices in them.

Emilia was then to meet them at the bottom of the main building, once she was able to get away from them. She had her powers to assist her, so she had reassured them she would be fine alone.

Without a moment more to lose, they split. Bailey and Noah took to the fire escape, they needed the more stealthy way in and easy way out.

Emilia took the stairs inside, twirling her dagger in her hands, preparing herself mentally for a tough fight. They had briefly seen what she was capable of, but she was stronger than she let on.

As she reached level three, there was an eerie feeling in the air, mutterings coming from one of the doors, and muffled yelling that could only be from

Taylor. Emilia tightened her grip on her dagger as she approached the door.

Emilia knocked loudly on the door, all noise from inside the room silenced, and she heard the familiar click of guns being readied.

After a second to build suspense, she kicked the door open and just as planned, all eyes were on her. Bullets were fired at her, and she dodged all with ease, letting her power guide her past them all. She trusted herself and her abilities, she had begun to master them after all these years. Soon she would likely be unstoppable.

It almost felt too easy, throwing them all about with her powers, slamming multiple guards into the walls with so much as a wave of her hand. Perhaps they were right to label her as dangerous, and advise against any interaction with her.

Amidst the chaos, she saw Noah sneak in through the back window, cutting Taylor loose and dragging her out, despite her pitiful protest - Emilia was handling everyone with ease and though Taylor would have loved to help, she wasn't a fighter, so she followed Noah out.

Bailey gave Emilia a signal from the fire escape, and she nodded and watched as he left. There was just one thing she needed to do before she left this place. Once the majority of the guards were down and dealt with, she grabbed one of them and pushed him up against the wall, holding her dagger up to his throat.

"Here's what's going to happen. You're going to tell me who the boss is around here and where I can find their office, I have a few questions before I leave."

"Alaric Vandona." The guard choked out quickly, clearly fearing for his life, he cried out. "He runs this place, he has a secret apartment on level four, just above here! In between office three and four there's a supply closet that leads to his office and the rest of his apartment is just past there! I don't know the code though."

"Thank you for your cooperation." Emilia let go of of him, watching as he crumpled to the floor in fear. Satisfied, she turned and walked out. Quickly heading up to the floor just above, where he had told her to go.

Surprisingly, he hadn't lied and she found the office he had told her about. She didn't need the code, she completely destroyed the door with her power. Inside, she found a map of Aglotar, certain locations circled, some crossed off. Next to the crosses was the world 'failure'.

It didn't sit right with Emilia and she kept searching, she had a few minutes at least while the others stole horses. One map near the top of the pile had Gold Dust Grove marked on it, they had found Connie's camp. Written next to it was 'take down rebel camp', with a date not too far in the future. Hopefully,

Emilia could warn them in time once Taylor was safe and away from here.

Something felt really wrong here. Everyone was under the impression that the Agency was there to help people, to rehabilitate and assist. Emilia now believed they had a more sinister reason to keep people with abilities and gifts close to them. No, the Agency was using people's powers, exploiting them for their own wrong doings, and defacing anyone that had abilities.

"You shouldn't be in here." Came a voice she hadn't heard in a long time. "This is very confidential intel."

Without wasting time he fired a bullet at Emilia, she moved gracefully and the bullet missed her body, instead making a hole in the glass behind her.

"Dodge as much as you like, but I have plenty of bullets and all the time in the world. You'll cooperate, or you'll die. I don't really care either way."

His voice was carefree, nonchalant.

"You need me, though, don't you? You want to open the gate yourself and it seems that I'm the key."

"Key or not, number thirty-seven, you'll either cooperate with me, or I'll just try and find a use for your dead body." A smirk crossed his face, and Emilia was caught off guard, a bullet hitting her this time. As soon as his voice uttered the number she had assigned all those years ago, the puzzle pieces began to fit into place. There was a reason she recognised him and it wasn't for anything good.

"I have to say, I am impressed how you somehow find a way to cheat death, maybe we need to look into that closer." He kept firing bullets towards her, and she managed to avoid the majority of them, letting them start to break down the large window behind her as she started to form a plan in her head, it wasn't a good one, but it was the best she had.

"Look around you, you've nowhere to go. Anywhere you go I will hunt you down and find you. When we're done with you we'll just use you as a training dummy, let new recruits kill you over and over again. It's good practice, after all."

His words were angering her. He had bolted the door shut and there was something in here limiting her powers - she couldn't seem to use them on him no matter how hard she tried, he laughed menacingly at her attempts.

"There's no way out, thirty-seven. Might as well give up now." Emilia looked out of the window, it was still a long way down to the floor, and no fire escape she could make a swift exit on either.

She took a deep breath, waiting for him to reload his gun, it was now or never. She swiftly grabbed the map of marked facilities and started to run towards the window. She crossed her arms, bracing herself for impact. The window was fragile from the bullets that had penetrated it thus far, and the second her weight was thrown at it, it gave way, splintering into hundreds of tiny pieces.

Emilia could hear him yelling behind her, gun shots firing and orders being barked, she assumed into a radio. The world went silent as she started to fall further down, the sound of her heartbeat was the only thing she could hear. Was this a crazy and stupid idea? Absolutely. Though Emilia had no regrets about her decision in the slightest.

As she plummeted towards the ground, she could hear voices calling her name, screaming them even. Emilia braced herself for the impact of the ground, but it never came. Her entire body was aglow with a familiar blue light, holding her not even a foot above the ground.

Then she heard the familiar sound of hooves hitting the ground, and a neigh cutting through the air that she would recognise anywhere, it was Onyx. Heads turned towards the sound, and Emilia let her body down to the ground before standing tall, reaching out to the mare.

"You always know when to turn up." She said to her, pulling herself up onto her back. "You're no normal horse, are you?" She received a grunt, almost confirming her theory. With no time to dwell on it now, she turned to the three people she cared about, who were speechless and unsure how to react. Emilia, however, was not willing to waste anymore time. "What are you waiting for? Rescue mission done, let's get the hell out of here!"

Twenty Three

They rode for as long as they could, but exhaustion had to come at some point. Emilia had taken them further north, up in the hills, and they were very lucky and found a cave at the base of one of the smaller mountains. Emilia promised to catch them all up to speed in the morning, when everyone had rested.

Tiredness was still a long way off for Emilia, so she insisted on taking first watch, allowing everyone else to sleep easily.

In the glow of the fire, she studied the map she was able to grab a hold of, trying to decipher where she had brought everyone. Hopefully, out of the way of danger.

At some point in the night, she came to an epiphany. There were no good guys or bad guys in this fight. The agency, the facility? They were all working together.

The Arcane Order of the Whispers.
The Afterward Censorship Heroes.

They were the same. No wonder both of the names were absurd, she sat there and worked out that they were each an anagram of the other, and it angered her that she hadn't realised it sooner, nor had anyone else.

What their goal was though, Emilia did not know. She assumed it had something to do with the gate Bailey mentioned. Why would they disguise themselves under a separate name, though?

She looked over at her little family, there were still some people missing. People that were in danger, and she had gone the opposite way. She had a quiet plan of getting them to the mountains and leaving them there, where they would hopefully be safe. Then she would be able to ride back south to return to Connie. Her heart longed for her safety, and the safety of everyone else there, Winnie, Jamie, Jackson and Myla, to the others that she had just started getting to know better.

"You have that look in your eyes again." Bailey whispered as he joined her side. "You're missing something, right? Or someone. You used to always have that look when you talked about home, your parents, Taylor. What's on your mind?"

"Connie's in danger, and everyone else down there. They've been labeled as a rebel camp, and that they need to be taken out." Her voice cracked. "Winnie and Jamie are so young, so innocent. They don't deserve any of this. And the agency aren't who they say they are. I'm angry, Bailey. They lied to you, Noah, Taylor. They lied to everyone."

He said nothing, just pulled her into a warm embrace, calming her down as best he could, placing a gentle kiss atop her head.

"I've had the joy of encountering Connie, on a couple of occasions." He said, "She's one tough cookie, she's stronger than she looks, you know? They've made it this far, I think they'll be just fine."

His words soothed her, but the emotions had taken over now that the adrenaline had subsided, she let her vulnerable side show. All she could do was cry into him, but he held her through it all. Emilia eventually tired herself out, and fell into a slumber while still being held by Bailey. He was a safety net for her, nothing bad would happen to her while he was around. Not anymore.

The Rebellion

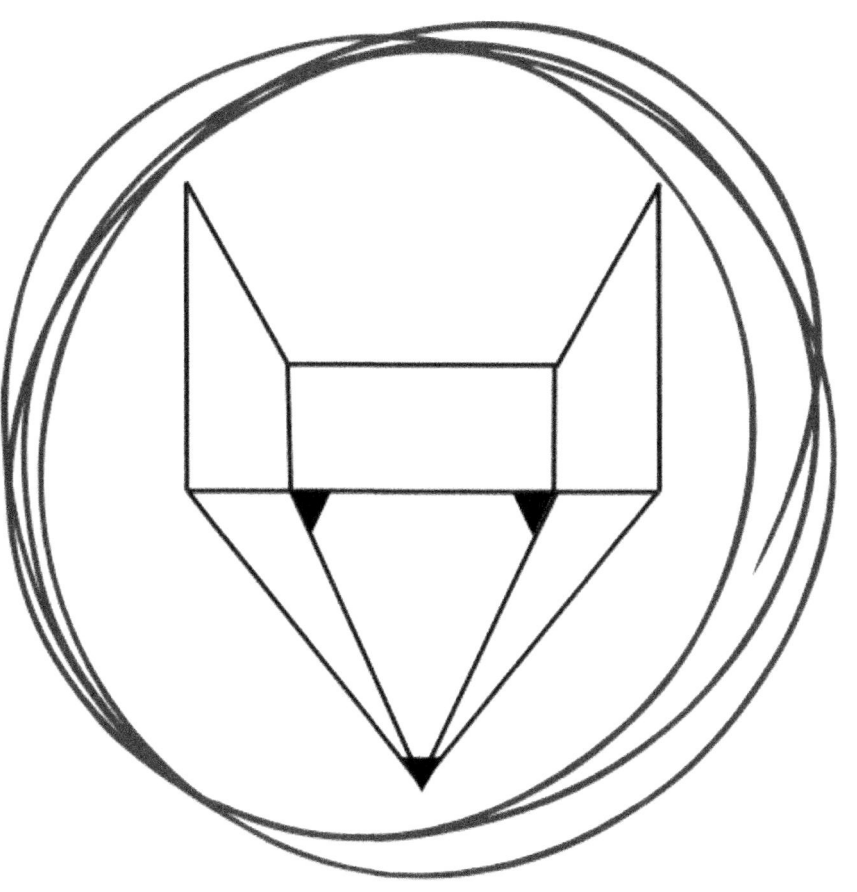

Ebratha

Twenty Four

"Absolutely not." Taylor demanded. "I have just found you again after years of thinking you were dead, and you expect me to just abandon you and go live in the mountains? Have you lost your mind?"

"You'll be safer there though, and I will come back after everything is over, I'll happily settle down up there too, live a simple life in the mountains? Sounds like a dream to me." Emilia countered, in a last attempt to persuade her. "Plus, you'll have Noah with you, it's not like I'm leaving you by yourself."

"Emilia," Taylor said softly, in a tone that reminded Emilia of her mother. "I don't think you've realised this just yet, so I'm sorry I'm the one to break it to you. This is never going to be over. They will look for you as long as you're alive. You said it yourself, you have to be the key to the gate, and they won't let up until they have you."

Always the voice of reason, Taylor's words made Emilia go quiet. She didn't want her to be right, but she was. It was highly likely that they weren't going to stop searching for her. At least not any time soon.

"We're all with you, Emilia." Noah chimed in. "I don't think any of us are willing to leave you now. Taylor trusts you, so I will too."

"I don't think I trust anyone more than you." Bailey spoke, his voice soft and quiet. "Everyone else has an ulterior motive, that's why wars begin. Someone always wants what the other has and they do everything in their power to get it."

Bailey took a step forward, towards Emilia, his green eyes honest and true.

"All you want is peace. I will follow you to the depths of hell and back again, because if that's the goal, I want in. I am tired. I'm tired of running, and being used, and being thrown about over and over again. I've had enough, and I'm sure there are so many like me that are tired of this life. So many of us that were forced into the facilities of the Whispers', or those that joined the agency, that were tricked into believing they were doing the right thing. Just like us."

The world fell silent as he spoke, the crisp air leaving all senses on edge.

"I say, that we help Connie and everyone else at Gold Dust Grove, and from there we start taking on every facility or agency we can. Save as many people as possible. Then maybe, just maybe we can all be free. You can show me your hometown, Emilia. We can build it back up together."

Tears had welled up in Emilia's eyes at his powerful speech. She herself, had never been great with finding the right words, but she could tell that it wasn't just her that had been moved by what he said.

Sharing a glance between each other, Emilia knew he was right. That they had to do this. It wasn't something they could just sit back and watch from the safety of the mountains, or some faraway town.

Emilia had promised Meladia that she would use her gift for good, and she would stand by that. Perhaps one day she could thank her in person for the gift she was granted. Though she may have despised it at first, it had become as much a part of her as the air she breathed or the blood that ran through her body.

"We need to be careful, take the back roads where we can, try and stay as hidden as possible." Emilia pulled out the map again. "They will likely expect us to take the main roads, because they are a direct link between towns and cities alike. If we take the more scenic route, it may be appear longer, but we'll likely save time and energy in the long run."

"Plus if we stay hidden, they won't know our location as easily so tracking us down will be a lot harder." Taylor said, tracing some lines along the map. "I've travelled with the agency for quite some time now, I don't engage in much of the combat, but they always need a medic on missions. I know a lot of the routes they take like the back of my hand."

Together, they decided to set off mid-afternoon, giving them chance to stock up on some supplies first and prepare themselves for the journey ahead of them.

Noah was indeed a skilled hunter, and he retuned within the hour with the prize of a fairly large wild goat for them to feast on before their long ride. Emilia watched with curious eyes as Noah carefully skinned and gutted it in preparation for cooking.

Taylor very clearly didn't enjoy watching this part as she had her back turned to her fiancé as she built a fire to cook it over. Surviving out here was not for the faint of heart, and even if she hadn't known about Noah's past experiences, it was certainly showing now.

It wasn't the worst thing Emilia had ever eaten, it was a little on the tough side, but it wasn't unpleasant. It was actually rather mild, and there was even a hint of sweetness to the gamey meat that surprised her.

With full bellies and all supplies prepared, they gather what belongings they had, though it wasn't much, and began their journey back south.

Twenty Five

Emilia was grateful that the journey was quiet, for the most part. Every so often, they would come across a small group of Whispers' or Agency members and would need to fight their way through to ensure news of their location didn't go any further.

None of them wanted to stoop down to their level and cause needless deaths, but they knew it wasn't really avoidable. When it did come down to that, they did everything they could to destroy any evidence that they had been there, hoping it would just appear to be another rebel group that had had enough.

Thankfully, they were able to avoid conflict for the majority of their journey because Noah was a wonderful look out. He was able to see things so far in advance that they often had plenty of time to divert before they were spotted.

Sometimes it was good to get the combat practice in, and they often found things that aided in their journey. Emilia's best find was a compass, which she kept on her person, using it alongside the map had made things considerably easier.

It took them just over two weeks to reach Gold Dust Grove, and it was like a ghost town. Emilia dismounted Onyx and walked through the deserted town. The sun was just starting to set, and the town looked beautiful.

It was situated in a spot where the light would cover it in a beautiful golden glow at dawn and dusk, hence where its name came from, but there was no one here but them to appreciate it, or so Emilia thought.

"Where the hell have you been?"

A gruff voice called out to her, and emerged from one of the small huts. Emilia didn't recognise him, he was lanky, with shaggy brown hair that was littered with an abundance of greys, though most of it was covered by a tattered dark brown hat that had seen much better days. Whoever he was, Emilia assumed he had been around a while.

"I did the best I could. Winnie and Jamie are safe with Myla, I sent them further South at the first sight of trouble. They're long gone now, hopefully somewhere more peaceful and away from harm. I had to bury Jackson, Rainer and Caleb alone, and they took Connie with them. Now, I'll ask you again. Where the hell have you been?"

His voice was filled with emotions, anger being a dominant one, and the only person she could assume he was, was Jep. Emilia was silent as she tried to put faces to the other names he listed off, guilt building when she couldn't. She had never met Jep, but Connie spoke very highly of him. Emilia wasn't nervous, despite his tone being very stand-offish, but she knew she had to answer him.

"I was, unfortunately, a bit busy being a hostage at the Censorship Agency."

Emilia spoke clearly, and the older man relaxed his shoulders a little bit, making him much more approachable.

"I'm sorry about Jackson, we were quite close while I was here. I didn't really know the others but I'm sorry you've had to do all of that on your own. Do you have any idea where they took Connie?"

The man shook his head solemnly. A look of defeat in his eyes.

"No." He sighed, "I'm sorry. I just know that they wouldn't have been able to take her if you would have been here. I tried making her go with Myla, but she refused."

"Yeah, that sounds like Connie." Emilia agreed, a sad smile crossing her face.

"Well, I suppose it's finally nice to put a face to the name, I'd say pleasure to meet you, Emilia, but I do wish it would've been under different circumstances."

"Likewise, Jep." Emilia spoke flatly, unsure of where they were going to go from here. This had been the first place they had planned on liberating, but they were too late.

"I'm going to try and find where Myla has gone with the kids. Might I suggest you don't stick around here, they come around every few days to see if you've turned up. They are looking for you everywhere. I don't know exactly what you've done, but you've certainly pissed them off." Jep chuckled wryly, it was obvious he wasn't pleased at the situation, but there wasn't much else you could really do in this kind of scenario. "I wanted to make sure I got to you before they did."

"I appreciate the heads up, Jep. Maybe I'll see you around when all this is over."

"Maybe." Jep repeated, sounding unconvinced. He raised his fingers to his mouth and let out a loud whistle, causing a horse to come to his side. He pulled himself up, but before he headed off, he gave a smile to Emilia one last time. "Good luck, Emilia. Keep in touch, if you can."

"He seemed nice." Taylor tried to lighten the mood as Emilia returned to them. "What do you want to do, Emilia?"

"What I want to do?" Emilia scoffed, "I'd love to find every single member of the Whispers' and the Agency and put them in the ground."

Everyone was silent, stunned by her words. Emilia sighed, rubbing her temples firmly, thinking things over. Trying to come up with a solution to everything all at once. All she could think about was the fact that there were three innocent people currently buried here, all because of her. How many more people would have to die?

Off to the side she could see the mounds of loose dirt. Jackson. Caleb. Rainer. She knew Jackson well, he had become a close friend of hers during her year here. She recognised the names of the others, but she wasn't close to them by any means. Eventually, she was able to tear her eyes away from the graves where they lay.

"No, what we're going to do is continue with the plan. We're going to find every facility and agency we can and take them down one by one. Jep said they took Connie, so maybe we'll find her in one of them."

Emilia pulled out the map as she spoke, figuring out which ones were closest to where they were right now. They had to start somewhere, and there was no time like the present.

"If you guys feel ready for it, the nearest one is only about an hours ride away. Strike in the middle of the night when they least expect it." Emilia felt rested, but more than that she had a fire inside her that needed an outlet.

Everyone was in agreement, and without a moment to lose they geared up and started to ride, headed straight for a facility. Emilia never knew she would be so willing and eager to return to a place that ruined her.

* * *

This one, wasn't underground, it appeared. So not all of them followed that same model. The plan couldn't be simpler; break in, free everyone inside, take down anyone who tried to stop them, and get out.

They were a force to be reckoned with, and with it being the middle of the night there were very few guards standing in their way. Any that were, were met with a quick end.

Emilia took the lead, using her powers to blast through doors, disable systems and quite frankly breeze through it. This was quite a small facility, potentially still quite new. It was all rather straightforward, and Emilia was almost begging for a fight to release some of her frustrations.

Together, they cleared each room, Taylor would always check everyone over for injuries and ensure everyone was okay as they left.

There was no sign of Connie, though based on the size, Emilia didn't really think she would be kept here regardless. If anywhere, she would likely have been taken to where Emilia had only just managed to break free from. Their biggest outpost, the one that took up a skyscraper in the large city.

The entire operation was over quickly, but Noah had found something to truly make their mark on the world. He had discovered a large amount of gunpowder being stored underneath, and he simply couldn't bare the thought of it being used to assist the Whispers' any longer.

Once everyone was out and safe, Noah blew it all up, and it took the majority of the building along with it. Something that showed that they were not to be messed with; a warning to the other facilities. The damage was done and the fire was the only source of light in the area. In it's own way, it was beautiful.

The majority of the people they freed immediately made a run for it. Emilia couldn't blame them really, they had quite literally done nothing but cause destruction.

There were some that stayed.

They were curious, some wanted to thank them. Emilia was surprised at first, in her reckless actions, she hadn't even thought about the aftermath for those that were set free during this mission. Some asked where they could go now, what direction their hometown was in, where their family was, why they saved them, why they were taken.

Emilia wasn't able to answer their questions, and very quickly she started to feel overwhelmed, her breathing getting heavier. She felt surrounded, felt trapped, and it terrified her to no end.

Bailey was watching her, for some reason everyone assumed she would have the answers to all their questions. He saw how much she was starting to panic, he felt it. He reached for his gun, firing a shot into the air. Everything fell silent, he had their attention. They weren't focussed on Emilia any longer. After a moment to compose himself, with all eyes now locked in on him, he started to speak.

"They call us thieves. Troublemakers. Rebels." He spoke loudly and clearly, his voice commanding attention and respect. It was captivating. "We stand for what is right. We fight for freedom. We fight for peace. They want to turn you into weapons for their own good. I spent three years in one of their facilities myself, I know what you've been through, and what you've been through is nothing short of hell itself. I was then recruited by The Censorship Agency, who lied to me. They tried to make me believe I was helping the world, but they are just The Whisper's under a different name, with the same goal. To weaponise you."

Everyone was silent as they listened to Bailey's speech, and Emilia stared in awe and disbelief at just how good he was at this.

"They want to make you into monsters for their own selfish reasons. I can't tell you how to find your homes or your families, but I can tell you not to trust any of those that tell you that the Agency is good. It isn't. You were all in there for one reason or another, whatever abilities you have, use them for yourself, no one else. I know you'll all do the right thing." Bailey's voice was getting quieter as he began to trail off. "You were all injected with a tracking chip when you arrived, if you are happy to let us remove it, please come see us. If not, do your best to find a way to get it out yourself. The sooner the better. Get as far away from this awful place at the first opportunity, run far and run fast."

There was a moment of silence after Bailey finished speaking, people digesting his words. Then, someone started to applaud. Before they knew it, everyone was cheering, clapping, celebrating. Revelling in their newfound freedom.

Bailey was taken aback by the response. As was the others, they were shocked at the response they received. Taylor, being the resident medic, was the one that helped remove every single tracking chip. She carefully secluded the area, slicing open where she could feel the tracking chip before delicately removing it.

Emilia was on hand to help heal the open wounds, ensuring that no one lose a horrific amount of blood in the process.

Noah would finish it off, cleaning the area and covering it with a bandage to help prevent infections. They had a nice flow going by the end of it, and everyone was so grateful to them, it filled them with immense pride.

When everyone had been seen to and headed on their way, Emilia and the others eventually set off to set up camp for the night.

Once the dust had settled and they had eaten and recovered from the evenings events, they were all quiet, all silently proud of their victory. It was surreal. Eventually, Emilia decided to break the silence.

"All in favour of Bailey being the spokesperson for the Rebellion?"

Immediately, Emilia, Noah and Taylor all raised their hands and laughter started to spread between them.

"You were so good, I could never speak to a big crowd like that, it was amazing!" Taylor praised enthusiastically.

"I just told them what I thought they might need to hear." He brushed off the compliment, almost shyly.

"Well, if you could keep doing that, it would be great, because I don't think I can deal with the questions afterwards." Emilia admitted. "There were some pretty young kids there, I hope they'll be okay."

Taylor scooted over to her friend, wrapping an arm around her.

"I saw most of them go off with someone older, I don't think any of them were truly by themselves. I think they'll be okay." She said softly, comforting Emilia's worried head.

"Thanks," Emilia smiled softly. "But the additional calmness you added with your powers weren't necessary, I can feel when you do it." She teased her, which made the slightly younger of them roll her eyes and scoot back to Noah.

"Well, I think we all did fantastic." Noah put forward his own opinion. "And I don't know about you guys, but I feel different. I feel amazing after doing that, like we really made a difference."

"Because we did make a difference." Taylor reminded him, leaning into her fiancé. "We have just saved so many people. I didn't see just how many ran off at the first opportunity, but even without them there were so many that stayed and let us help them. We've accomplished something truly meaningful tonight, we deserve to be proud of ourselves."

Everyone could sleep soundly that night, and they needed their rest because this was just the beginning of it all. They had a lot more work to do, as this just marked the beginning of the rebellion.

Twenty Six

Over the next seven months, they made their mark across Aglotar. Their rebellion was growing. The more people they freed, the more people that knew about them. Of course, the people they saved would sometimes spread the word with good intention.

Bailey spoke to the masses after each success, creating an exciting atmosphere. It wasn't just him that grew their reputation, Taylor was very popular among people. She had a calm and kind demeanour that people needed, and her empathetic nature made her the one to go to for anything people needed, even without her powers she was an inspiration to them.

Not only that, but she was growing stronger too, and was very successful with helping people revive lost memories. The hope it spread was wonderful, people knew where they were from and a rough idea of how to get there. People remembered their families, their friends, their homes.

They often had to get creative with how they would take down each place they came across, often depending on the supplies they had and what was contained within the facility, and Emilia just kept checking them off of the map once she had the moment to.

They often passed through towns, filled with those they had freed from facilities and agencies alike. People sometimes felt indebted to them and provided them with shelter for the evening, or a warm meal to aid them on their journey. It was kind, and greatly appreciated, and it was becoming more common the longer they continued their mission.

Sometimes, when passing through a town, they would often stay for a few days and help people understand their abilities more. Some people were overwhelmed, and unsure what to do with themselves now that they weren't being told what to do all hours of the day. Some, like Bailey and Emilia, had been in there for years and needed a gentle hand to guide them back into civilisation.

It was scary. Bailey and Emilia knew this more so than Noah and Taylor, and it was clear that they had a soft spot for anyone they saved from the facilities. It wasn't just physically difficult in there, but they mental toll it takes was one that could last a lifetime. Even now, Emilia still awoke in the night expecting to be trapped within the steel bars, in the damp, cold cell that she was told to treat like a home.

Their revolution inspired others to follow a similar path, and slowly, there was a shift in numbers. While those in charge of the Whispers' Facility and the Censorship Agency still had a greater amount of power, and wealth, the rebels weren't going down easily. Word was spreading all across Aglotar, and now into Roanloch.

People had started to associate the small group with the like of foxes. They were sly, quick, often struck in the late hours of the evening, and of course, Taylor's auburn hair mirrored the colour of a fox's fur. Bailey may have been the first face of the Rebellion that people saw, but it was evident that the one people remembered was none other than Taylor.

It was because of this, that they had started to see drawings of foxes more often, especially in towns that helped them. It was a subtle nod to show which side they were on. Even just the colours were starting to become iconic; white and orange. If anything it fuelled the group even more so, encouraging them to continue their journey across all of Ebratha.

Emilia couldn't remember when, but they were on Roanloch grounds once more, and though it didn't look massively different to Aglotar, it felt different. That may have just been because she grew up on this side of the split so it naturally felt more like home to her.

They were in between locations at the moment, the four of them were strong together and almost unstoppable, and they were running out of marked locations. For quite some time now they had been having to do their own intel to try and locate more of them as the ones that were left were few and far between.

* * *

The sun was high in the sky, it was mid to late afternoon, and they had just been talking about taking a little break soon, maybe making a stop at the next town they came across to try and update their map, perhaps find some potential new locations..
"Nevermind, armoured van in the distance guys. This is new." Noah informed the others. "Looks like they might be taking people from their homes. I've not seen this before."
"Maybe that's how the Whispers' get people now." Bailey retorted. "I say we go and put a stop to it, what about you guys?"
In agreement, they began to speed up, in order to catch them before they were done and gone. What they saw was startling to them, they were taking people, some by force. Though they couldn't truly say they were surprised, they had seen their lack of morals, so this wasn't out of character for them really.
What struck a chord most for Emilia was how young some of them were, it's like as soon as they start showing any signs of abilities they take them, regardless of their age. One she saw couldn't possibly be older than eight years old.

As soon as they were spotted, the guards started finishing up, very swiftly getting into the armoured vehicle and starting the engine. Clearly they didn't want a fight, and based on their reaction alone they knew exactly who they were up against.

They were shot at as the van drove away, and counter fire was provided by Noah and Bailey. Of course, they were on horseback so they had to be careful that the horses didn't sustain any major damage, so Emilia tried to provide a shield for them, but it was hard to keep up while she was also trying to fight back at the same time. The van sped up, leaving most of them in the distance, unable to match the speed of the van.

Not Emilia and Onyx though.

Onyx pushed through with ease, Emilia still wasn't sure exactly what she was, but she knew she was far from a normal horse. At the moment, even the impossible was possible, so she wouldn't be surprised if some animals were affected by the war. Together they kept up with the van, and Emilia came up with a plan as quickly as she could. It wasn't without flaw though, and she only planned so far.

"You're pretty good at finding me, aren't you." She swallowed the lump in her throat, taking one hand off of the reins and using her powers to open the back door of the van, where she could see everyone inside.

She couldn't ask them to jump out, they were moving so fast that the kids wouldn't dare to do it, and if they did they would most definitely be injured from the fall, which Emilia didn't want to risk. She pushed Onyx even further to where she was almost level with the van. "I'll see you at some point, Onyx, I'm sure you'll bring the others to me, too."

After another deep breath, Emilia held up her palm, channeling all her energy to try and slow the truck in it's tracks. It worked just long enough for her to leap from her steed and into the back of the van, letting the doors shut close again afterwards. They had to know that she was in there, and she would face the consequences for that when the van came to a stop.

Out of curiosity, she tried to open the van doors again, and they wouldn't budge. Emilia tried using her powers, but her light didn't even fully emit, it merely sparked, of course they had found a way to dampen any abilities. Couldn't have people escaping now, could they?

The Whispers' Facility

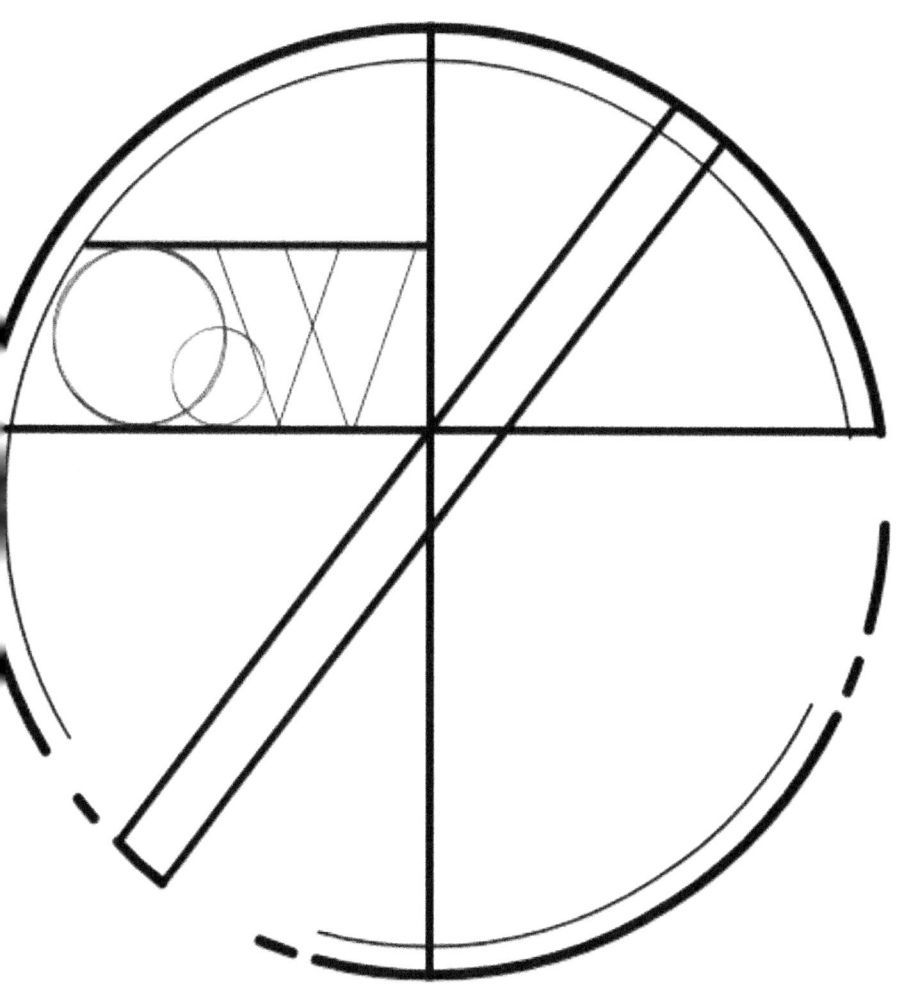

Ebratha

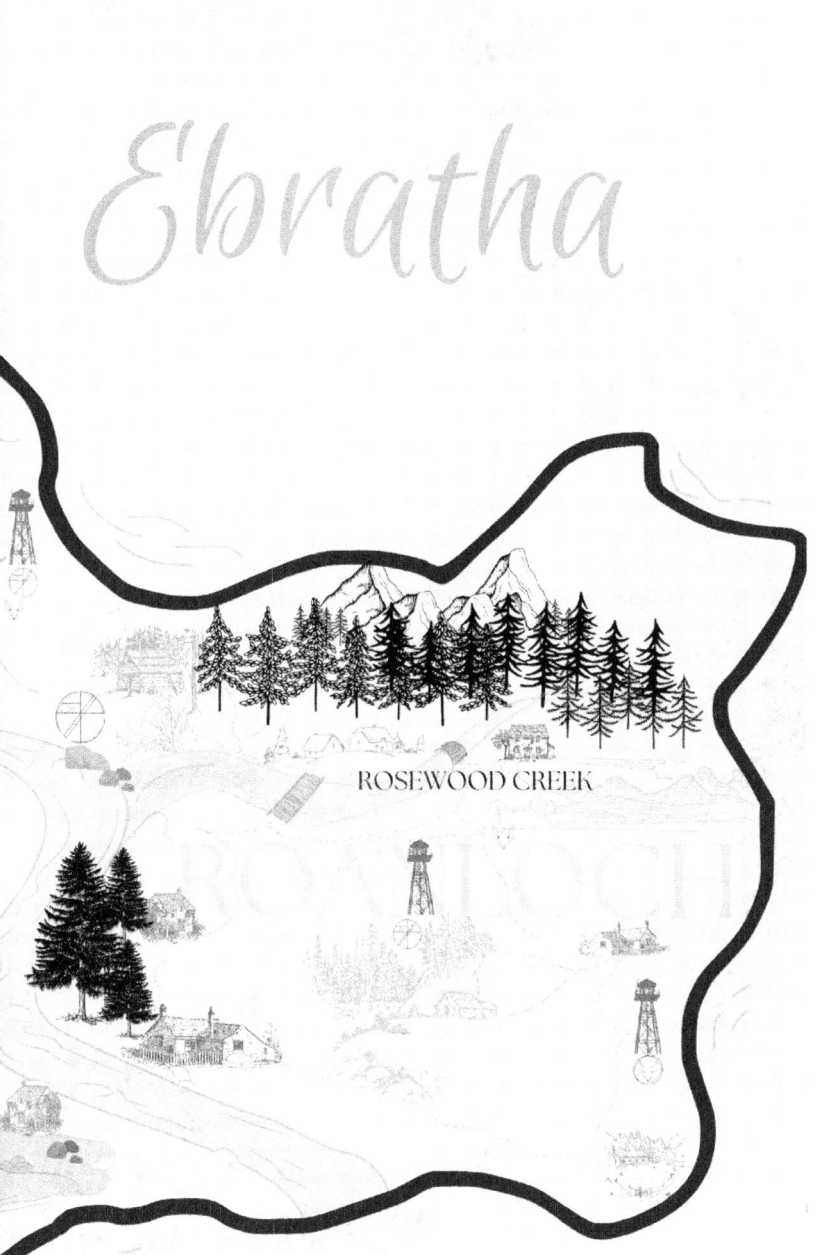

Twenty Seven

Emilia was in the van for quite some time, the children in there were silent, they were terrified. Even the ones that were slightly older, almost teenagers, didn't say a word. Emilia was about their age when she was first brought in, if not slightly older, and she would have been just as scared.

Never the best at words, Emilia wasn't able to comfort them or reassure them. As much as she wanted to tell them they would be okay, she didn't want to make false promises, nor could she bring herself to lie to them. Instead she stayed silent herself, trying to think of a way out of this mess. Her powers weren't working as they should in here, and it worried her.

Eventually the van came to a stop. Emilia rose to her feet, ready for a fight, ready to protect the young kids that they had taken. It was morally wrong, on so many levels, and she wouldn't stand for it.

The door didn't open. Instead, the back of the van started to fill with a grey, smoky gas. Emilia fought it for as long as she could, but it took her down eventually, and she was greeted by the familiar darkness of unconsciousness.

It was hard to tell how much time had passed, but Emilia opened her eyes to see reinforced bars, which faintly buzzed, leading her to the impression that they were electrified.

She reached over to her arm to see if they had replaced the tracking chip, but it appeared that they hadn't bothered this time around, though she was unsure as to why.

"Oh, you're awake!" A young voice chirped from the side of her. Emilia turned her head to see a very young girl, she was dark skinned, not unlike the warmth of copper. With light brown eyes that had some almost golden tints in them, and dark brown hair that was almost black, but not quite. It was tied in two low bunches, keeping it away from her face. "Why did you jump?"

Her voice was timid, but inquisitive.

"I wanted to try and save you all." Emilia tried to choose her words carefully, but she didn't want to twist the truth. "These people that took you, they're not nice. I'm going to try and get you all out of here as soon as I can, okay?"

The young girl nodded at her.

"Okay. My name is Amana, what's yours?"

"My name is Emilia. Are you hurt?" She asked, trying to see if the young girl had any injuries on her. It broke Emilia's heart how young she looked, she couldn't have been older than ten at the latest. Amana shook her head.

"No, I was pretty lucky actually, I got away with just a few cuts, but my mama always said I heal pretty quickly."

Emilia smiled softly at her, feeling protective over the little girl.

"We'll get you back to your mama as soon as we can, okay?"

Amana didn't look as sure.

"I don't think my mama is there anymore." She said in a quiet voice, clearly upset by the thought so Emilia didn't push her further.

Having lost her own parents in a tragic fate, she could emphasise with her, her heart still breaks thinking about how scared they must have felt that day, and yet they did everything the could to ensure her own safety, calling home to make sure she was there and knew what to do.

"Well, I'm still going to get you out of here and get you back home, whatever it takes. My friends are really smart, so if I can't get us out of here, I'm sure they'll be able to." Emilia reassured her with a gentle smile. The girl, however, didn't seem too worried. She had a very calm aura about her, despite the events that had happened today.

This place appeared to be much stricter than the facility Emilia started out in all those years ago, further security was in place, and she could only assume it was partly her doing.

Emilia didn't quite know where she was, or how far away she might be from Bailey, Taylor and Noah. She was hoping they might be able to find her quite quickly, but she couldn't take the chance of just sitting and waiting, she had to come up with a way to escape herself.

The hum from the electrified bars was like white noise to Emilia, almost calming her nerves. She didn't fear these places as much as she used to, but her powers, unfortunately, weren't working as they should within these walls. She wasn't quite sure why, so she opted to save her energy instead. The only thing she could assume is that there was something in place to dull people's abilities, clearly they had the technology to do so from what she witnessed in the van.

Amana was fixated on Emilia, and whenever they were away from their cells the young girl stuck close to her side. Emilia didn't mind, really. If anything she was growing quite attached to her, she had a wide eyed curiosity that Emilia missed about herself.

Over the next week or so, Emilia had done her best to put together a few ideas for a plan. This particular facility was rather small, but it appeared to be focused on certain elements. Emilia had noticed that there was always canisters being transported throughout the halls; potentially their biggest trade.

Perhaps whatever elements within those canisters, were being used to suppress people's powers. It made perfect sense in her head, but she remembered that as she wasn't in Aglotar anymore, and Roanloch wasn't exactly known for it's scientific findings.

Surely she would be able to use that to her advantage, so she did her best to research into them. Whilst this place didn't exactly have a library full of knowledge, it did have plenty of people. Some, that knew a bit more than others.

As it turns out, her instincts were partially correct. Most of the canisters contained flammable gases, some containing propane, ammonia, carbon monoxide. Whilst she didn't know if they were being used to repress abilities, she knew what flammable meant, and she could use that to her advantage.

The rarest one that they traded was one called chlorine trifluoride. Emilia had been informed that this one was in fact the most flammable out of all the ones they traded. Its as rare, and only came about every few months, but it was so powerful that it would be able to take town this whole place with ease.

Apparently, she wasn't the only one who was looking into burning this place to the ground. Emilia had befriended a couple of people with the same goal as her, they would make a great addition to their group when they got out. Lorenzo was hyper attentive to their schedule and had it all noted down in a code only he knew, to ensure it wasn't noticed by any of the guards.

He was a shape shifter, but they had put a limiter on him to stop him from changing form when he wasn't in training. Come to think of it, most people had been forced to have limiters in place, but given that this entire building seemed to be emitting something that essentially nullifies everyone's abilities, it was a bit pointless.

Then, there was Gracie, she was very eager to leave at the first potential opportunity. She was very conservative with her powers as she didn't want them to know just how powerful she was, but she was a master of the natural elements, her favourite form was creating flames, which Emilia made a mental note of - it would be such a shame if those flammable gases met Gracie's fire.

Not only that, but Gracie was very sneaky. She had been slowly but surely discovering secrets about this particular facility, and how it hid supplies away in secret corridors and rooms that were hidden away from the naked eye - it reminded Emilia of how Alaric Vandona had a hidden apartment at The Agency Headquarters.

Every now and again, Gracie would find something of interest and manage to slip it away without anyone noticing. She was rather good at creating distractions and making things disappear. The amount of guards she had gotten into trouble must have set a record by now, if only they knew it was her.

Emilia had been given access to her stash, which included just the things she was looking for, marked locations of other facilities, agencies and small camp settlements where they had soldiers stationed. It was like she had struck gold. As she flicked through the different papers, she felt exhilarated, like a new wave of life had breathed through her soul.

Up until she came across an envelope with words she wasn't expecting to see.

Gold Dust Grove.

Emilia's felt her heart drop, she felt dizzy, nauseous. She took a deep breath, sitting down to have a look inside.

There were pictures of everyone inside, including herself. Pictures of Jackson and Connie had a cross on them in red marker, and she assumed the worst, that is until she saw there was writing on the back of each photo. On the back of Jackson's picture was simply the word dead. However, on the back of Connie's picture was the word taken.

Connie was alive, or at least at the time of them putting together this envelope, she was. There were notes about herself, too; that she was incredibly dangerous, that people were to shoot on sight, not to engage alone. Thankfully, there was nothing in here about her family. No pictures of Bailey, Noah or Taylor. She felt a wave of relief wash over her.

That relief was short lived, as Emilia started to realise that the soldiers here must know about her. If they knew about her, and hadn't tried to kill her again meant there was another reason that she was being kept here. One she didn't want to stick around and find out for. One that she didn't want her family to be lured into.

Maybe that's why they were keeping her here unharmed, maybe she was nothing more than bait. The thought alone made her stomach churn, it made her angry. It was then that she decided it was time to force an escape. No waiting for the right time; she had to make it the right time.

Twenty Eight

It was almost as though they knew she was planning something, because the very next morning, before everyone was escorted to breakfast, they came down to her cell, with armoured soldiers, informing her that she needed to go with them.

She didn't particularly want to, but Emilia wasn't faced with a choice. Amana, who was in the cell next to her, looked scared for her. Emilia gave her a soft smile, "Don't worry, it'll all be okay." She whispered to her, giving her a small sense of reassurance before complying with the guards and going with them.

It was obvious that they were all apprehensive to be around her, as they all kept their distance and kept avoiding eye contact with her. It made her feel powerful, and in usual circumstances she would be able to take them all down in no time at all. Even if she just had her dagger, she would be able to break free from them with ease.

These were not usual circumstances, though, and she did not have her dagger, or have her usual powers. It was frustrating, but all she could do was keep going. She had studied Gracie's map of this facility time and time again, so she had a rough idea of the layout, and all of the secret compartments it hid. She was very aware of one that was actually a secret way out, but it was impossible to get through. There was nowhere to input a code, no keyhole, nothing. Neither Gracie nor Lorenzo had figured out how to access it, they would be long gone by now if they had.

If she had her powers back, Emilia was sure it would take nothing more than a wave of her hand and she would be through. Her powers had only grown stronger over the past year, she was doing everything in her power to grow where she could - always keeping Meladia's words in mind. Surely this is what she meant, she was using her abilities for good. She was saving as many people as she possibly could all across Ebratha.

Eventually they took her into a rather small room, it was an interesting layout; the room was divided. On one side, were people who appeared serious, intimidating. However, the bags under their eyes intrigued Emilia, something had to be keeping them up at night. The were behind a control panel, separated by a glass wall.

On the other side of the clear divide, was where Emilia was being taken in to, and in front of her was a strange contraption. At first glance, it looked to be a chair with an arm rest and a foot rest, but upon further inspection, they were restraints on each section, and a very peculiar machine hooked up to it.

Emilia was forced into the chair and secured tightly at all areas, her arms and legs were strapped tight to the plastic-like material that covered the seat. She hated every second of this, it was humiliating, dehumanising and she had never felt more powerless in her life.

Then, someone else walked into the room. Someone she recognised immediately and couldn't resist the urge to roll her eyes.

"Number Thirty-Seven. How nice of you to join us here." Came his low voice, dripping with sarcasm.

"The pleasure is all mine, Vandona." Emilia retorted in her own sarcastic tone. "What took you so long?"

"Well, once we found you I had to come all the way out here, to lovely Roanloch." He scoffed, clearly unhappy with having to make such a journey. "You've made quite a mess of Ebratha, Emilia. Single handedly, you've taken down some of my biggest outposts and infiltrated so many of my facilities and quite literally burned them to the ground."

Emilia couldn't help but feel a sense of relief again, so far, Alaric hadn't mentioned anything about Taylor or Bailey or even Noah, all of them had been agents hired for him at some point, yet he didn't even seem to acknowledge their existence. She was glad, though. It meant they hadn't been caught yet, either that, or he was withholding information from her. She chose hope, and believed in the former, at least for now.

"However, I am willing to let it slide on one condition. You tell me where the gate to the other realm is, and I will let you walk away from this."

A silence filled the air, and Emilia stared at him blankly, confused.

"The day we found you, was the same day that a gate appeared in one of my facilities, an archway made up of a bright blue light, people were able to walk through it, but they never returned. I can only assume they perished, I have never heard otherwise. Then you showed us your power, that same blue light was within you, we assumed you would be the way in."

As Alaric spoke, explaining everything, Emilia was quiet. Taking in his every word. She knew very little about this, only learning of its' existence from none other than Bailey.

"We had such high hopes for you." He tutted, shaking his head in disappointment, like Emilia needed the additional disapproval. "But you just kept fighting us. Not only that, but soon after you started showing these marvellous powers the gate just… Vanished. Gone without a trace and we have yet to find it since.

Alaric brought the machine beside her to life by pulling a large lever down. It lit up, and started to whir. Mere seconds later Emilia could feel a shocking sensation go through her body. This must have been the shock therapy Bailey mentioned all those years ago.

The two of them went back and forth for quite some time, Alaric kept increasing the voltage to cause further pain the more she resisted.

"I don't know!" Emilia gasped out in pain, unsure of what else she could do to persuade him. "I didn't even know about the gate until I ended up at your Agency!" She snapped at him, wincing through the pain, doing her best to push through it.

Alaric turned off the machine briefly, clearly frustrated in the lack of progress that had been made. Emilia took it as a chance to catch her breath, start recovering from shockwaves still resonating through her veins. He gestured to someone in the other room, and an image was projected onto the blank wall.

Connie.

"Maybe, just maybe, you'll be a little more cooperative if you knew that a certain someone's life was on the line?" He taunted her, the video as clear as day before Emilia.

She was thinner, and covered in bruises, but it was Connie. Emilia's emotions were spiralling, feeling everything all at once. Anger, sadness, joy, fear. Emilia knew she needed to pick one, so she settled on anger. It was often more powerful than the others, and she needed adrenaline to get her through this.

"So that's it, you took her just to use as bait to get me talking?" Emilia snapped at him. "Well you're out of luck because it won't work. I don't know where any gate is or was."

Emilia already knew her words weren't going to be believed at any point this evening, so instead she focussed her energy on trying to work out how to escape and get out of this place. Connie was alive, and that was what mattered right now. She didn't want to call his bluff, but even if they did find the gate, they would need Emilia's cooperation to use it so it was highly unlikely they would kill Connie right now.

"Hm." Alaric grunted, signalling again to someone in the other room. Someone spoke into a receiver, a few moments later the video caught Emilia's attention once again. "Maybe this will change your mind."

Emilia was given no choice but to watch as someone started to beat Connie with a baton of sorts, a tool chosen likely for the fact that it wouldn't immediately cause bleeding - something they could use for a while without killing the recipient. At the same time, Alaric had brought the machine back to life, yet again increasing the voltage.

However, Emilia noticed something. Each time the level was increased, there was a shift in energy. Sometimes a light might flicker above her. This machine was using a lot of power from the facility. Which meant it was directly connected to the facility.

An idea was starting to form in her brain as she suffered through the physical and mental torture they were putting her through.

Twenty Nine

"Sir, it's almost at full capacity, it'll kill her if we keep going." A soldier informed Alaric, who appeared indifferent to the result. He just shrugged.

"If she doesn't know, she's no good to me anyway." His voice was devoid of all emotion. "If she survives this, just rinse and repeat until you get an answer. I have other rebels to deal with. Mr Larson has caused quite a stir near Havron and I need to clean up that mess before it gets out of control. Once that's taken care of I'm getting out of this side of Ebratha and going back to Aglotar."

His words were clear in their intentions, to try and break Emilia even more. When he saw it didn't change anything, he left, briefly speaking to the people in the other room before he left.

Emilia was absorbing every ounce of electricity that flowed through her veins, the machine kept going for some time after Alaric left. Everyone in there was shocked at how much she was able to take, and even though the soldier was clearly apprehensive to turn it up to full force, Emilia was excited.

Unsure as to whether her idea would even work, she knew it was now or never. Emilia clenched her fists tightly, shutting her eyes and taking a deep breath. She imagined the electricity leaving her in a sudden burst, forcefully repelling it. As she persevered, she heard everyone mumbling, and people started to get frantic around her, she didn't know what was happening, just that she needed to keep going.

Suddenly, the room went black and there was a loud bang. At first, Emilia thought she had passed out, but the emergency back up lighting came on moments after, illuminating the way out. All the restraints that had bound her were burnt off, barely even a trace of them being there.

The people that were in here were on the ground, their bodies limp and fried. Clearly, electrocuted. Emilia was amazed, but didn't want to stop and stick around for someone else to find her. She heard a commotion from outside of the room, shortly followed by gunfire.

Bursting out of the room, she realised that people were making a break for it. The power outage must have unlocked all cells, but not only that it had stopped whatever they had been using to dull everyone's powers.

"Emilia!" Came a familiar voice, and a petite hand dragged her away from the bustling crowd, it was Gracie. "This has you written all over it, are you okay?!"

The younger girl was frantic and ecstatic, clearly ready to run, she started to pull Emilia in the way of the crowds. Emilia resisted, planting her feet firmly on the ground. She was met with a look of confusion from the teenager.

"We gotta go, Emilia, they'll have the power back on in no time, I'm sure, we have to take the opportunity while we have it. Lorenzo has gone another way to see if we could find you, we're meeting outside of the facility as soon as we can. We have to go!"

Emilia shook her head.

"I'm going for Amana, she'll be scared. I promised I'd get her out of here." Emilia meant her words, and Gracie could already tell that there would be no convincing her otherwise and nodded. Emilia smirked a little. "Plus, I intend to use that flammable gas to blow this whole place up, meet me at the secret tunnel entrance in five minutes."

"But that door is sealed shut with no way to open it!" The girl argued back at Emilia, looking over her shoulder, just wanting to run.

"With my powers, I can open it. I know it. Please, I can't leave Amana."

"Okay," Gracie nodded, pulling Emilia into a tight hug, just in case before jogging off in the direction of the exit.

Emilia, on the other hand, started to make haste the opposite direction, back to where she knew Amana would be.

As she reached the familiar sight of her cell, she spotted her. The gate was loose and unlocked, yet Amana sat in there still, pulling her knees up close towards her chest, making herself as small and unnoticeable as possible.

"Time to go, Amana." Emilia said softly as she opened the cell door completely. The little girls head perked right up as she heard Emilia's voice, throwing herself at her and grasping her tightly. Emilia wrapped her arms around the young girl, and she found herself smiling, relieved. "Come on, there's a secret way out." Emilia held Amana's hand so she didn't lose her, though most of the chaos had subsided now, there were just a few stray soldiers that didn't stand a chance against Emilia now she had her powers restored.

Together, they arrived at a round, metal door with no keyhole, no keypad, not even a door handle. Gracie was already there, and had clearly been trying to find a way to open it. She stood back at Emilia's instruction and watched as Emilia raised her free hand at the heavy door, closing her eyes and focussing. After a few seconds, there was a mechanically clunking and the door unlocked, slowly swinging open. She pulled Amana into another tight hug.

"I'm closing it after you've gone through. As far as we know, there's no other door after it. Gracie, you said that you think it brings you out near the river, I'll meet you both there when I'm done."

Emilia was met with Amana's eyes that looked to be on the brink of tears.

"You... You're not coming with us?" She asked, her voice back to the timid tone that Emilia was used to.

Shaking her head, Emilia smiled sadly at her.

"I have something here I need to finish up, to make sure they don't hurt anyone here ever again, which is why I'm closing the door, to keep you safe. It's going to be loud, and scary but just keep going, okay." She looked over at the teenager with a pleading look. Gracie knelt down to Amana's level, offering an open hand for her to take. "Gracie is a really good friend, you'll be safe with her."

Reluctantly, the little girl agreed, but didn't leave without one last tight hug. Emilia watched as she started to walk down the dark tunnel, with the only light coming from Gracie's free hand, a flame emitting from it.

Emilia felt herself getting emotional as she watched them start to leave, Amana kept looking back, which didn't help. Eventually, Emilia forced the door back closed, sealing herself in once again. Not allowing herself time to dwell on those feelings, she sprung into action, and made her way down to the weapons store. She would need something to assist her with the explosion. A simple match would have likely done the job, but she found something that would create a much bigger bang.

She left the weapons storage with her dagger that they had been keeping hostage, and a grenade.

The next few minutes went past in the blink of an eye, finding the supply of gas canisters was easy, especially from the amount of times she had studied Gracie's maps of this facility. Emilia spread them out across the different rooms. In each room she placed them, she loosened the valve ever so slightly, just enough so that the gas inside started to escape at a slow pace.

She wanted to do her best to leave no trace of this place, making a large circle and ending back where she started.

This was something she wasn't sure she could survive, which is why she was happy that Amana left with Gracie. At least she had someone, just in case the worst case scenario came to life.

Emilia dampened some cloths she had found, on the off chance that she did survive, there was bound to be a lot of smoke in the aftermath, which she needed at least some protection from.

In the middle of the room, Emilia placed down the last canister, once again loosening the valve and releasing the gas inside.

The whole facility must have been starting to fill up with gas now, and it was time to give it the spark it needed. Emilia made a break for a small compartment in the room, which she assumed was a supply closet based on the cleaning materials in there.

Emilia took one last deep breath, before she pulled the pin on the grenade and threw it into the room. She pulled the supply closet door closed and braced herself for the impact.

Thirty

Emilia shut her eyes tightly, the damp cloth and her dagger just on the floor in front of her. She covered her ears, and leant forward to try and brace herself for impact. The next few seconds felt like a lifetime. The noise was so loud she couldn't hear anything at all.

She could see the bright blue light through her squinted eyes, and she put all of her energy into shielding herself throughout the explosion, just hoping Gracie and Amana were far enough away to be safe.

Emilia's loved ones were all she could think about; Connie, Bailey, Taylor, Noah, her parents. Until now she never believed people that claimed their life flashed before their eyes. Emilia found herself back at Rosewood Creek, watching the sunrise with her mother by the end of it.

"It's still not your time, love."

Her mother's voice was calm, kind, loving. Everything she needed to force herself back to reality. Opening her eyes, she saw there was no longer a door where there used to be. Destruction surrounded her, and the flames were hot. Emilia reached out in front of her, one hand grasping the damp cloth, the other securing her dagger.

Thick smoke was all around her, it clouded her vision and made it near impossible to breathe. She had to get out, and she had to get out fast. Emilia knew there was an emergency exit somewhere near her, but she was so disoriented that she could barely tell up from down.

Stumbling across the room, she followed whatever light source she could see that wasn't caused by the flames. She came across a sign for a stairwell, but the door wouldn't budge.

Emilia beat her fists against the door. She threw her weight at it time and time again. It barely even creaked. She was exhausted; the shield she used to protect herself during the initial explosion had to be the most draining thing she had ever done.

Collapsing to her knees, tears streamed down her face. She didn't know of any other way out right this second, and she only had so long before the thick smoke would take her under. Emilia didn't want it to get to that point, she couldn't safely assume she'd survive it when she was unconscious and unable to use her powers.

She sheathed her dagger into the holder attached to her waist, taking short, laboured breaths. Emilia swallowed before letting out a scream, raising her hand at the door. A blue light emitted from her open palm, forcing the door to burst open.

Emilia threw herself through the door and started to sluggishly climb the mountain of concrete stairs, pushing her body further than it wanted to go.

Freedom was within her reach as she saw the fire escape sign. She used the wall as support as she pulled herself up from the ground, standing on her own two feet. She pushed open the exit and the sunlight streamed in.

Emilia stepped out onto what appeared to be a flat roof. Somehow she had climbed up two stories, she hadn't even realised this place had two stories; all maps they had only ever showed the ground floor. She gulped down the fresh air, the damp cloth long gone by this point.

Still lethargic and struggling, Emilia did her best to make her way to the edge of the building. She saw conflict. People fighting. On one side was the uniformed soldiers of the facility, the others, she wasn't sure at first, but then she saw Bailey.

"Bailey." Her voice croaked out, hoarse from the near suffocation. They had found her. Emilia didn't know how, nor was she going to question it. Further down, she saw where all of their bins were stored, and Emilia dragged her body towards it.

It wasn't pretty, but it was the better option than just throwing herself straight off of the building without anything to break her fall.

The light didn't help her like it had back at The Censorship Agency, but her life was in much more danger then. This was only two stories up, and the bags filled with waste cushioned her fall. Emilia hardly noticed the smell as she dragged her body out of the bin.

Everything was loud, and she had exhausted her abilities, her body, mind and powers were all utterly burned out.

Carefully, she managed to stand up. Hoping that she would be able to make it down to the river unnoticed so she could ensure that both Gracie and Amana were safe. She knew that both Bailey and Noah were very capable and Emilia wouldn't be able to help them out right now even though she wanted to.

Emilia was ale to make it around the corner of the building without passing out, and she could see where the river was up ahead, a few hundred feet away. She knew she could make it if she pushed through, but a voice stopped her in her tracks.

"Emilia!"

Turning around, she saw the familiar, friendly face that was Taylor and Emilia managed to smile through the pain. Knowing her friend would be able to help her accomplish what she had set out to do, so even if either of the younger girls had been hurt, Taylor could help them.

As Taylor was rushing towards her friend, the sound of a gunshot filled the air. The smile on Taylor's face was gone, replaced instead with shock. Time stood still for Emilia as she watched her friend fall to the ground, a pool of blood slowly forming around her body.

Emilia was filled with rage when she saw Alaric's nonchalant face behind her. He took his time reloading his gun, giving Emilia chance to run over to Taylor. The puddle of blood was rapidly growing in size and Emilia could feel the tears flowing down her cheeks.

Both her hands were over Taylor's body, partially trying to stop the blood flow, partially trying to get her powers to work.

"Come on!" She shouted in frustration, over and over again.

A hand clasped over her own, it was Taylor.

"It's okay, Emilia." She spluttered out, "It's not your fault."

Even in her last breaths, Taylor was still not thinking of herself.

"No!" Emilia cried. "No. No. No. No. No!"

The words kept falling out of her mouth, though she wasn't able to form a single sentence. The only family she had left in this world was fading away from her right before her eyes.

Emilia raised her head when she heard the familiar click of a gun. Alaric had the weapon pointed right at her, but hadn't fired it just yet.

"Go on then!" Emilia yelled at him, clutching Taylor's body, refusing to let go. "Do it already! I've had enough of fighting! What are you waiting for?"

Her words were filled with anger. Filled with hatred. Eventually she heard the familiar sound of the bullet being fired.

Emilia let out one last scream at Alaric, her words intended to hurt him. Before the bullet made it's mark, Emilia's light was back again. Not to shield her, but it fired upwards in a large beam of light, that reached a pinnacle and exploded, blue light falling down in a dome shape from the sky, encasing everything around it.

Time stood still.

Thirty One

Noah had seen everything. His body felt numb, and he was blindsided with rage. Then, he witnessed the light being emitted from Emilia and how everything just slowed around him. Behind him, came the familiar whinny of Onyx, heading straight for Noah.

The mare nudged him on approach, almost pushing him towards the two women. Noah looked over again, Emilia's body was weakened by whatever she had just done, and she was laying on the ground next to Taylor.

Noah rushed over to them both, able to move with ease, yet everyone around him appeared to be frozen in a moment in time. The bullet was still in mid air, on it's way towards Emilia. He pulled Emilia up, and laid her onto Onyx's back, her body was limp, but he managed.

The sight before him shattered his heart into tiny shards. His fiancée, the woman he had loved for years, was laying before him, drenched in her own blood, her body lifeless. He scooped her body up in his arms, tears streaming down his face.

A gentle nicker came from beside him and he nodded, still clutching Taylor with everything he had. Noah looked around, and there was a very slight movement from the world around him, the light above them all growing dimmer by the minute. He knew, that whatever Emilia had done was starting to wear off.

Suddenly, another beam of light appeared in the distance, a beacon in the twilight hour. Atop of Onyx, he started to ride towards the light, leaving this cursed place behind them. He had on hand on the reins, the other holding Taylor close to his body. He knew Emilia had healing powers, and all he could do was hang on to the last bit of hope that it wasn't too late.

The ride was slow, and the time dragged on into the night. Once they got close to one beam of light, it would start to fade, a new one forming further away. Noah just kept following the light, hoping it was leading them somewhere safe, somewhere far away from danger.

Eventually, it was the only light they had, so they had no choice but to keep going. He felt bad for leaving Bailey behind, but he too had been frozen in time. Noah wasn't sure as to why he had been able to move, but he decided that it was best not to question it. Bailey knew how to handle himself, though, he would be just fine.

There had to be an end somewhere, and Noah assumed they had found it. They reached one beam of light, but there was no replacement to be seen. He didn't know where they were, just that they were in a forest of some kind, near a lake, too from what little he could see. He took both girls down from Onyx's back, who must have been exhausted by now, and laid them down gently on the ground.

Noah kept talking to Taylor, hoping, praying she would be okay. Telling her that Emilia would fix everything when she came to, that she would be okay. It was more like he was trying to convince himself, even though Taylor's heart had stopped beating before they had even set off. He tried to restart her heart multiple times. He applied whatever her could to cover the open wound. Noah was running out of options and ideas.

Sleep didn't come easy, it was more like his body surrendered every so often just for a short period of time before his mind awoke him yet again. It went on all throughout the night, but finally Noah saw light start to appear. Slowly, but surely, golden rays started to filter through the leaves on the trees and Noah felt the sun's warmth on his skin.

It wasn't just him that was arising though, as he saw Emilia's body start to move, regaining it's consciousness.

* * *

Looking around, Emilia was met with confusion. It wasn't the first time she had lost consciousness in one place and awoke in another, but it wasn't that she was confused about. She was confused because this place felt familiar to her, yet she didn't know why. Her heart hurt as she saw Taylor's body next to her.

"I tried all I could to save her." Noah's voice was heavy. He was hurting badly, Emilia didn't need Taylor's Empath powers to know that much. He looked as though he hadn't slept a wink. "I did everything I could to stop the blood flow, and keep her safe. I failed."

Noah could barely take his eyes away from the ground, ashamed in himself. Emilia put her arms around him.

"No," She said softly. "You didn't."

"Yes, Emilia, I did. I promised to protect her and I failed. She's dead. There's nothing we can do to change that."

Emilia didn't want to believe that, so she tried her very hardest to bring her back. Her powers were strong again, but they weren't enough. It just wasn't meant to be. Noah watched her frantic actions from afar, not really wanting anything to do with it now.

"She's gone, Emilia." His voice was broken, defeated. "She's gone."

"No!" Emilia shouted, angry at the world, at herself, at Noah. "It's not fair! It's not fair!"

Emilia was in a slump next to the body of her best friend. Knowing, that if she hadn't jumped into that van, then she wouldn't have been at that facility. If she hadn't been there, then Alaric wouldn't have come all the way over. If Alaric had just stayed in Aglotar, Taylor would be alive.

"I'm going to kill him." Bitterness swept through her body, a feeling she hadn't been well acquainted with before; vengeance. "The next time we come across Vandona, he's mine."

"We'd have to find him first, and that would mean finding our way out of these woods." Noah reminded her, looking around again. 'We're in here pretty deep by the looks of things, it was so dark last night when we came here."

"Why did you come here then?" Emilia retorted, "Why not go somewhere that we weren't going to be lost?"

"I thought you had a plan!" He snapped back at her. Emotions were running high for both of them. "I didn't really know what was happening, so I just followed one light beam and then another appeared, and then another. You brought us here, not me!"

"I was unconscious, Noah!" She yelled at him, unsure of when they had both rose from the ground to be standing, but they were face to face now. "I'm sure it's so so hard to see a million miles away but my power takes a lot, and I mean a lot of actual physical effort. You think I can just magically create beams of light when I'm not even conscious? It's probably another trap, one you rode us straight into. Well done, Noah, time to go again with the torture. I can't wait!"

"That's enough." Came third voice that silenced both of them. "That is enough from both of you."

Emilia and Noah both turned to look at where the third voice came from, to see a being that looked so ethereal, regal and magical.

"Meladia." Emilia's voice softened instantly, surprised to see her again. "How are you here?"

Meladia smiled knowingly, brushing her long, wispy hair off of her shoulders.

"Why, I live here, Emilia. Just as you once did."

The realisation hit Emilia, there was a reason this place felt so familiar to her; she was home. She turned quickly, taking in her surroundings before dashing in one of the directions, quickly making her way up to the edge of a hill, one that she knew well.

She watched as the sun started to bring light upon her town, one she barely recognised. The buildings were mostly rubble and ruins, the river that once ran through it which brought such life was all but dried up.

Deserted. Her small town that was once so full of vibrancy was abandoned. Empty. A shell of the town it once was. Sitting on the edge of the cliff, she took it all in, she hadn't set foot in this place in years. It looked nothing like she remembered.

Before long, she was joined by Noah, who took a seat next to her on the cliffside. Emilia couldn't help but lean into his body, she needed the physical comfort of another but didn't quite know how to ask.

"I'm sorry, Noah. I'm sorry I yelled, I didn't mean any of it."

"I know, Emmy. I know." Noah whispered, wrapping an arm around her, letting her in. "I'm sorry, too."

Rosewood Creek

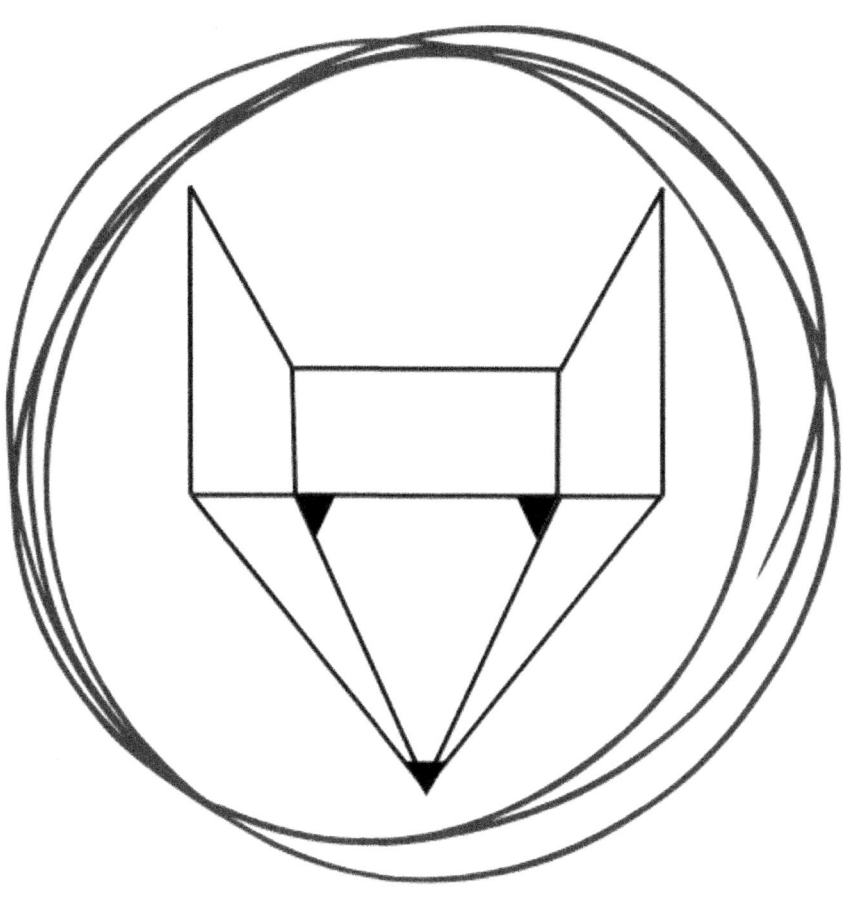

Ebratha

ROSEWOOD CREEK

HAVRON

SAFE HAVEN

Thirty Two

The next couple of hours were surreal for both of them. Emilia had told Noah previously about Meladia, but this was the first time she had been face to face with her. Emilia could only handle so much at one time, so she decided with Noah to deal with one thing at a time. The first thing she wanted to address was Taylor.

Walking back through her town felt unnatural. The pathways that once were surrounded with beautiful greenery and flowers were still recovering and there was very little life right now.

They reached Emilia's house first, or what used to be her house. There wasn't all that much left on the surface, so Emilia decided to try the bunker. Someone had been through, clearly. Maybe even lived down here for a time. Maybe it was Taylor at some point.

There were some supplies left, some canned goods that were still edible, water, medical supplies, and something they both decided was needed for the time being; her father's alcohol. Eden didn't drink often, it was reserved mostly for special occasions and celebrations. Emilia found a large bag along the way that she started placing items in.

After all they had been through, and for what they were about to do this evening, they deemed it a necessity. They also made the trip over to Taylor's old home. It was a little further out than Emilia's house, so it was able to withstand a little more wear and tear. It was still a wreck, but it at least resembled a house.

It was almost too much for Emilia inside, but she got through it. She also came across multiple family photograph albums - she had also picked some up from her house before they left - and placed them in her bag with everything else they had gathered.

With supplies and shovels in tow, they returned to the forest. Meladia confirmed upon there arrival that there was nothing that she could do about Taylor, she offered her sincerest apologies. Emilia had a feeling it must have been hard for her too, really, she had watched both herself and Taylor grow up from what she had told her.

Emilia suggested the grassy spot atop the hill, Noah didn't seem to care anymore. He looked distant, and she could understand why. Sometimes the emotions were too much to handle, and the easiest way was to completely detach yourself. Emilia knew that feeling very well.

They worked in silence as they took shovels to the dirt, until they had a hole big enough. Emilia went over first, she wanted to make Taylor look a little more like herself once more. She cleaned her up, brushed her hair and straightened her clothes, making her much more presentable.

Noah carefully carried Taylor from her previous resting spot, up the hill and laid her gently in in the hole in the ground. Emilia could hardly look at her best friend. She was so pale now, her body limp and lifeless. It was crushing her.

"Flowers." Emilia finally spoke up. "We can't bury her without any flowers."

Noah nodded, and the two of them gathered a beautiful collection of wildflowers that grew in these woods. Back in silence again. Ever since she regained consciousness, she had only heard Noah speak a small handful of times. It wasn't completely out of character, but it hit much different now. They scattered the wildflowers in with her, though reserving some to place on top.

Noah was still silent as he leant in close to her, resting his forehead on hers for a few minutes, his eyes closed tight. He hesitated as he pulled himself away, it was clear as day that he really didn't want to. Placing a long, tender kiss on her forehead, the tears started trickling down his face again. Noah reluctantly stood aside to let Emilia go in for her last goodbye.

Emilia swallowed the lump in her throat as she moved in, sitting down next to her best friend.

"You know I've never been the best at words. You were always the creative one, the art you'd make, the stories you would tell. I could never do that. I will never be like that, and that's okay. That's what I have you for. Had."

She took a shaky breath.

"You know I don't like goodbyes, I really don't. So how about see you later? We all have to go at some point, I know that. I think I'm just angry that it happened so soon. It wasn't even a year ago when I found you again. I remember it like it was yesterday, I was so happy to see you, see that you were alive and well."

Emilia wiped away the tears from her face.

"You were so happy. You were always so happy. You always saw the bright side when all I saw was darkness. You were my neighbour. My best friend. My sister. And I'm going to miss you more than I think you'll ever know. I braided your hair, just the way you like it. I hope you like it, anyway."

She played with the end of the braid a little more, just neatening it up, moving a stray flower from away from her face at the same time.

"You were too young for this. For any of it, and you didn't deserve it. I'm sorry I couldn't save you. I just... I need you to know I tried. We both did. You've helped save so many lives, so many people are safe and happy because of you. So many people love you, everyone we set free all seemed to adore you anyways, it's not hard to see why."

Emilia choked back another sob.

"For god's sake, if only you'd have stayed in the mountains with Noah you'd be alive right now. I'm sorry, Taylor. I love you, I love you so much. I'll see you again at some point."

It was all Emilia could manage before she started to break completely.

They started to bury here under layers of dirt as the sun began to set again, the day drawing to a close. Emilia carefully placed the last of the wildflowers atop the grave, her face red and puffy.

They took a seat near the cliffside again, Noah decided it was time for her dad's reserves. He opened the bottle, taking the first swig. It was a long drink that he took from it before passing it over to Emilia, who followed suit.

It was a sweet honey mead, quite easy on the palate but very dangerous because it never tasted strong, but it was. They passed the large bottle back and forth between them for some time. Noah had been trying his best to put on a brave face for the majority of the day, but he let his guard down now and his vulnerable side was truly showing.

Emilia held him tight while he got it all out of his system, letting him cry as much as he needed. When all was calm again, they laid back on the grass, looking up at the evening sky.

"I understand why you miss this place, it's so much nicer than the cities in Aglotar." Noah managed to get out eventually. "Even the air feels different. More natural."

"We always tried to work hand in hand with nature, me and Taylor would spend so much of our time in these woods. She loved it. She could sit for hours just drawing every little creature she would see, the different flowers you'd find, and everything in between."

Emilia smiled, though there was a sadness to her words.

"I don't know if I can stay here, Noah. It feels wrong now. Like I don't belong or something, I'm not sure."

"Don't be ridiculous, of course you belong." He rolled his eyes at her. "You belong here as much as the sun belongs in the sky. This is your home, Emilia, don't ever think differently."

"Home is where your family is, in my experience. This last year, my family has been all over Ebratha and everywhere we went could be home if we wanted it to be. But now, everyone has split up, I don't know where most of my family is now. There's a little girl that I met in the facility there and I need to find her. I promised I'd keep her safe, that everything would be alright." Emilia sighed, knowing that it would be an impossible task to find her, maybe Gracie assumed the worst and took Amana under her wing. As long as she had someone, that could maybe be enough for Emilia. Noah rested a hand on her arm, silently reassuring her.

"I'm sure we'll be able to find her. You're pretty good at that, you know." Noah encouraged softly. "We were talking about having kids soon, when everything settled down and the war was over."

"I'm so sorry, Noah." Emilia spoke quietly, solemnly. She sat up again, taking another long drink of the mead before handing it over to Noah. "I'm going to miss her smile. She had the brightest smile and she was so full of kindness and optimism."

"Yeah, except for when she hadn't eaten." Noah managed to throw Emilia off guard and they laughed, just a little, though it quickly faded as Noah looked over to her grave. "I'm going to miss everything about her."

"Me too, Noah."

Thirty Three

Birdsong filled the air, a soft breeze rustling through the leaves above where light was filtering in from gently started to wake Emilia. Then came the bleat of a goat.

Emilia sat up swiftly, and the sight before her completely bewildered her. It was Daisy. She reached out to scratch her behind the ears, just where she used to love it. The goat leaned in to Emilia's touch. Shaking her head in disbelief as she realised how much her little goat had grown in the past few years. Honestly she was surprised that she had survived.

Her head hurt from the night before, and her mouth was as dry as a bone. Emilia looked over, Noah was still in a deep slumber. She let him sleep, he hadn't had much the night before.

Stretching out her limbs, she stood to her feet, Emilia felt restless, like there was so much that had to be done. For years she had longed to be home once more, yet now that she was here all she wanted to do was run.

Emilia filled the hole in her stomach with some of the goods they had gathered yesterday, retrieving the photo albums that her and Noah had gone through under the light of the moon. There had been a lot of tears and emotions as they looked through the years upon years of captured memories.

Not being able to bare it any longer, Emilia took herself for a walk through the forest, Daisy trailing just behind her. It helped her to clear her head. She wound up at the lakeside where she first came to, and there was still blood staining the ground where Taylor had laid.

Moving on, she followed the river upstream, until she came across a small waterfall. The sound of the water crashing onto the surface soothed her and she took a few deep breaths, calming herself. She could feel movement around her, and she knew who it was without even needing to open her eyes.

"Hello, Meladia."

"Hello, Emilia." Came her melodic tone. "When you and Noah are ready, I need to speak with you both. I understand that you are mourning, but it is rather urgent."

Emilia nodded in understanding, not wanting to waste any time she decided to go and retrieve Noah. Thankfully, he was already awake by the time Emilia made it back to the cliffside.

She relayed Meladia's message to him, and Noah agreed to speak with her immediately, they both longed for a distraction. His eyes landed on the goat just behind Emilia and shot her a look of confusion.

"This is Daisy." Emilia pointed at the goat, her voice quiet. Noah closed his open mouth, his lips pursed as he tried to think of something to say but nothing came. He just shrugged in acceptance.

Together they returned to the waterfall, where Meladia was waiting for them patiently. The two of them stayed silent, waiting to hear from the ethereal spirit of the forest.

"I appreciate you both coming so soon, this couldn't wait much longer. The veils between worlds is wearing thin, and I am very weary that the shadow creatures we call The Nox Malum will be breaking through before we know it."

Meladia paused, as though remembering a time long since past, and Emilia gasped as she put the missing pieces together.

"I knew it! I knew that book wasn't just an old fae tale!" She felt revitalised, and it had surprised both Meladia and Noah. "There's an old tale, The World Beyond. It was my favourite book, but everyone always said it was just a story."

"Ahh, yes." Meladia smiled knowingly. "There is only one copy of that book, Emilia. I planted it very early on, when I knew you would be the one to take over after my time came. I'm pleased that you enjoyed it as much as you did."

Meladia turned to face Noah, who wouldn't be familiar with the tale.

"I came to this world a very long time ago, I swore to protect it from the shadow creatures, but my powers kept fading over time. I knew I would have to chose someone to gift my powers to in due time, I chose Emilia. There are people in your world that are trying to bridge the gap between this world and others, and it's weakening the thin veil of protection that has been put over your realm."

"I thought they had found a gate though, one that appeared the day my powers came alive." Emilia countered. "It wasn't something they made."

"No, but ever since then they have been trying to replicate it and find a way, they are starting to succeed. It's really only a matter of time before the gate is opened."

"I don't understand, Meladia. How can they be nearly succeeding? It's magic. It's not something they can scientifically replicate and make themselves. Like any of the powers I've seen, surely they have no logical answers that can be solved with science, right?"

"That is correct, Emilia. However, you are well aware that you are not the only one with gifts. Abilities have been gifted across your world by my peers. They briefly crossed over a long time ago and selected a number of souls that would inherit their abilities during the upcoming war.

The Nox Malum are relentless, they destroy everything and create a darkness wherever they go.

Emilia, you are a Protector, you always have been. Somewhere in your world, there is a Gatekeeper. If you don't find whoever it is before they do, no one's world is safe."

Both Emilia and Noah were silent, taking in the information as best they could.

"Ebratha isn't exactly small." Noah's voice came out quieter than usual. "How would we even go about finding someone like that?"

"Now that is something I can help you with." She gestured to the small waterfall behind them. "It's not quite a gate to the other worlds, more like a window. I can't say exactly what you'll see, but you will come out much different than when you first entered. Emilia, I believe that if you enter you will see what you need to."

Emilia watched as the water crashed onto the surface below, then looked back towards Meladia and Noah. Taking a deep breath, she pulled her shoulders back with pride and nodded before walking towards the water.

"Good luck, Emilia." Meladia whispered as she watched the young woman wade further in. The water cascaded down, covering her from view until she was no longer visible to either of them.

"Will she really see something?" Noah asked skeptically, the disbelief obvious in his voice. "You said she would not come out the same as how she went in, is that really true?"

"Of course." Meladia admitted softly. "At the very least, she won't be as dry as she was before she entered. Anyways, come with me, Noah, I have something for you, too."

Thirty Four

The water was cold as it hit her back as she went further into the waterfall. It was almost like going through a tunnel, as it stopped as she walked further into the darkness.

There was nothing here, it was just darkness surrounding her. It felt strange, and she still felt as though she was underwater despite the evidence around her proving otherwise. Emilia tried to focus her mind on finding the Gatekeeper, which was surprisingly difficult due to how much she had on her mind currently. Trying to fixate on just one particular thing was a near impossible task.

The sound of a heartbeat slowly started to sound out. Emilia pushed her feet to move as she started to follow the sound. As she approached the sound started to speed up, steadily getting faster and louder the closer she got. She burst through an invisible wall and she found herself away from the darkness.

The colours were dampened, desaturated, but the place was alive with movement. Laughter and chatter filled the air, and Emilia wandered around the village surrounding her. She quickly learned that no one here could see her, she was nothing more than a ghost right now. Nothing was obvious as first, anyone in this village could have been the Gatekeeper. Emilia once again tried to focus on the word and idea of what it entailed. The town around her shifted, like time was passing before her and the vibrancy was dulled even further.

Laughter and chatter no longer filled the air. People were slouching more, they looked tired. Something had happened here, it was clear as day to Emilia.

Suddenly, there was gunfire and screaming.

Emilia's feet moved before she even had a chance to think about her actions. Not that she could do anything to help, all she could do was watch. What she saw made her nauseas.

Amana.

She watched as Amana was dragged away from an older woman, the similarities in their faces was uncanny. It was obvious they were related, whether she was an older sister or mother, she wasn't sure but she was assuming the latter based on the fight she was putting up.

Emilia could feel the heartache, the pain in her screams as Amana was forced away and thrown into the back of the van. A van that she recognised.

There was hurried movements, and more gunfire. Most of that pointed towards the rebel group that Emilia was leading. However, she couldn't take her eyes off of the older woman, and she saw that she was bleeding out from a bullet wound.

Emilia walked over to her, ignoring the van and her former self that was chasing after it. She crouched down next to her, not wanting her to be alone in this.

"I'm going to find Amana, I'll try and bring her home, I don't know if she has any other family here but if she does I'll find them. If not, she can come with me, and I'll do everything in my power to keep her safe. I promise."

She vowed sadly, not expecting anything of it. Suddenly, the woman's head moved, catching Emilia off guard. Her eyes were the mirror image of Amana's.

"Please, keep my daughter safe. They can't know. They can't know what she's capable of. Please."

The words sent a chill down Emilia's spine, and she agreed without hesitation, nodding her head, and stayed with the mother as the life quickly faded from her eyes.

It had to be Amana. Maybe she didn't even know herself, but she had to be The Gatekeeper.

Thirty Five

Noah followed Meladia, trusting that Emilia would be safe, at least for now. They didn't venture too far away from the waterfall, and he could still hear the crashing of water even now.

"I truly am sorry for your loss, Noah. I know this is a difficult time for you." Meladia started, choosing her words carefully. "I know that Emilia trusts you with everything she has, that much was obvious when she chose you to bring her here."

"I don't think she chose me, she was unconscious after whatever it is she did." Noah stated, confused by the words.

"No, Noah. She picked out someone she could trust while unconscious. She saw you and knew you were the one to bring her here." Meladia corrected. "Either way, I know your soul is good, Onyx wouldn't have let you come otherwise. She's from my world, I brought her here as a foal. I also brought Selenite."

Meladia led him to a horse that was white all over, and was the epitome of elegance.

"He has been separated from Onyx for quite some time now, and these horses bond for life, he's been very eager to return to her but we needed the time to be right. After all, I had sent Onyx to watch over

Emilia when she was taken. If you'll have him, he's all yours. I know you'll take good care of him."

Noah looked shocked, he cautiously approached and gently stroked the horse's neck.

"I would be honoured. Thank you."

"You're very welcome, Noah. I have also strengthened your bow, very beautifully crafted, may I add. I have also given it a light enchantment to assist you, but from what I have seen you are a very skilled archer and you don't need it, but it's there regardless."

Noah was speechless, looking over his bow, it didn't appear to look any different, but it felt different. He struggled to untangle his thoughts and find words of gratitude. He looked up at Meladia, who had a proud smile on her face.

"I have one last thing for you, Noah. Come." She gestured for him to follow her. He walked after her until they reached a small clearing in the woods. "Emilia and Taylor spent many afternoons right here. I'm not sure how long I'll be able to hold her spirit here for, but you'll have at least a few minutes, if you would like."

"A few minutes for what, sorry?" Noah asked as he looked around the clearing, not seeing anything out of the ordinary.

"A few minutes to speak with her again." Meladia's voice was lower, almost saddened. "I understand if it's too much much right now, but I don't know how long her spirit will be around for. Some fade a lot faster than others."

Noah swallowed the lump in his throat, blinking back tears at the thought of Taylor.

"No, I'd love to see her again. Even if it's just a second."

Meladia nodded, taking a step away from Noah. She closed her eyes and after a few seconds, Meladia's body faded away.

Noah watched in awe as she disappeared in front of his very eyes, and out of habit he clasped his hands together, popping his knuckles to ease his nerves.

"Hello, love." Came a sweet, familiar voice from behind him. He turned around and the tears started to trickle down his face as he saw Taylor. She had her hair in the braids that Emilia gave her before they buried her, but she had colour back to her face and she looked radiant.

Noah reached out to her, to pull her into his embrace, but his hand went straight through hers and he remembered that she was nothing more than a spirit.

"I miss you already, Tay." His voice was weak, this was harder than he thought it would be. "I'm sorry."

"My love, you have nothing to apologise for." She tried to tell him.

"I was meant to protect you, keep you safe. It should have be-"

"You and I both knew the risks we were taking, Noah." She gently interrupted him. Reaching a hand out to wipe away the tears running down his cheek. "I'm not in any pain, love. I know what you and Emilia did, thank you for bringing me home."

"I hate this." Noah whispered. "I hate that this is the last time I'll see you. I hate the fact that I couldn't do anything. I just can't believe you're gone."

"I'm not gone, I'm not going anywhere. I'll always be with you, Noah. I don't think this is the end. I'll see you again, when the time comes. Just promise me one thing, though." Noah met her eyes, nodding, willing to do anything she would ask of him. "Don't be alone. I know Emilia is struggling too, I see it in her eyes. Stay with her, don't let yourselves get lost, okay?"

Noah nodded, trying once again to put on a brave face, he stood with pride again, nothing that had happened had been his fault, nor Emilia's.

"Thank you, love." Taylor smiled, taking his body language as an agreement. She placed a kiss on his forehead, though she may have only been a spirit now, Noah still felt her gentle touch and treasured it. "I have to go now, I'll be watching over you guys, okay?"

"No," Noah muttered, trying to grasp on to the moment to stop it fleeing. "I'm not ready. I can't do this without you."

"You can." Taylor reassured him as she started to fade away. "And you will. There's still so much to be done, but you'll be okay, love."

"I love you."

"I love you, too."

A large splash, followed by gasping brought Noah back to the reality in which they faced. He left the clearing and returned to the waterfall to see Emilia on her knees in the middle of it.

Shortly after he got there, Meladia returned, checking that he was alright, Noah nodded, and thanked her once again, grateful to see his fiancée even just once more.

"So?" He called out to Emilia, "Do we know where we're going?"

"We have to go back." She told him, panting as she left the icy cold water. "Back to the place I just blew up. Do you remember which way it was?"

"Maybe, but it was dark and I was just following the beams of light, but I think we came from the West."

"Amana's the gatekeeper. Maybe. I think." Emilia's uncertainty didn't fill Noah with confidence. "The waterfall took me back to the day I jumped into the van, but before that. I saw her mother, she asked me to look after her. Said that they can't know what she's capable of."

A gasp from Meladia turned both of their heads towards her.

"You were able to communicate with her?" She asked excitedly, "You're getting so strong with your powers, Emilia."

Her words made Emilia smile shyly.

"Thank you, I don't really know what happened, but the kid doesn't have family to go back to, I don't think." She informed Noah solemnly. "She's one of us though, which makes her a target. We have to find her. Before Vandona does."

* * *

They prepared to leave, not wanting to waste any more time. Noah caught Emilia up to speed on what she had missed while she had been in the waterfall as they gathered their belongings and tacked up the horses.

A familiar guilty feeling was rising in Emilia, she was leaving Daisy behind again. A part of her knew that she would be fine, though. She had survived this long, and there was always a possibility that Meladia was helping look after her. Emilia gave her a hug before she left her home once again.

"You were right though, Onyx isn't just any horse. She's from Meladia's homeland. So is Selenite." He patted the horse's neck as they finished up and prepared to leave. Before they left, Emilia returned to Meladia one more time.

"What do I do when I find her?" She asked cautiously.

"When the time comes, you'll know what to do."

"But what if I don't? I never know if I'm making the right choices or not. I feel like I just keep making things worse." Emilia countered, she was scared, everything was getting more serious. The stakes were higher now, and the consequences sounded terrifying.

"Emilia, you have come so far from when I first spoke with you. You're doing just fine. I promise, when the time comes, you'll know."

Emilia nodded in understanding and said her goodbye to the eternal being, not knowing if or when they would see each other again.

"What's the plan, then?" Noah asked her as they set off.

"First, we find Amana, Bailey and a couple of other friends I made in there, hopefully they're all safe. From there, I'm not quite sure just yet, but I'm sure I'll figure it out."

Thirty Six

Atop Onyx and Selenite, it only took a few hours before Noah could see the wreckage in the distance, which they headed straight towards, not wanting to waste any more time than they had already.

The area had been abandoned, it seemed. It made Emilia feel quite sick as she saw the amount of fallen bodies around this place, there were a lot of facility soldiers in their uniforms, but also a lot of people who had no uniform.

Both sides had casualties, both sides lost a number of people. People whose names would likely be forgotten, and their families - if they still had them - probably wouldn't even know.

Thankfully, there were no bodies that neither Emilia nor Noah recognised. Both of them had done enough mourning for now. There was no sign of Amana, or Bailey, or anyone else for that matter, which worried Emilia.

They eventually ended up right at the side of the building, and they patrolled the perimeter of it, and eventually something caught their eye.

Emilia's dagger.

It was jabbed into a wooden post, keeping a piece of paper in place. Emilia retrieved her dagger, placing it back into it's holder attached to her waist. She was grateful to find it once more, but the note it was holding left her feeling uneasy.

> If you want to see your friends again, come see me in Havron. I'll be waiting.
> A. Vandona.

Emilia clenched her fists, trying her best not to destroy the note as she did so. Frustrated and unable to speak, she passed the note over to Noah for him to read.

"I don't even know where Havron is, but I do remember him mentioning that Bailey caused a bit of a stir over there." Emilia thought back to the day she received the shock therapy, but she couldn't remember him mentioning anything else about this place.

"I'm not completely sure myself, Emmy. It can't be too far away though, we were making out way through Roanloch before you were taken. Maybe one of the local towns know about it?" He suggested as he tried to find it on his map, but unfortunately the map they had didn't have a lot of information on the towns and villages in Roanloch, it was more focussed on the locations in Aglotar.

"I think that's probably the best idea, can you tell where the nearest town is on that map?" Emilia asked, peering over Noah's shoulder to see if she could see anything. "I know there's a village a little ways South of Rosewood, it's not very big though and I don't even remember what they call it."

Noah shrugged, putting the map away.

"I'm happy to follow you, Emmy, this map doesn't really have any information about Roanloch. I don't think The Agency haven't been over here as long as they've been in Aglotar."

Emilia smiled softly, appreciating the trust he appeared to have in her. Granted, it had been a long time since she had made a journey to the neighbouring towns and villages, and she had never made the journey herself before, she had just gone along with her parents, but in her soul she believed she could do it.

Both of them were eager to leave the devastation and wreckage behind them, silently mourning all those that had been lost.

It only took them a few days before they saw a small town take shape in the distance. They were both feeling hesitant as they approached, unsure of what kind of welcome they would receive. Emilia hoped that at the very least they weren't hostile towards them.

They slowed their pace as they reached the town, it wasn't the busiest place they had seen, but people were out and about, minding their business in the town square. The buzz of chatter was constant but never loud. It was surprisingly normal. It reminded Emilia of home.

They had dismounted and loosely tied their horses to a post in the middle of the town. Noah looked a little uneasy, like he wasn't used to the crowds.

"You alright?" Emilia checked in with him gently.

"Yeah, I just didn't expect it to be this busy." He admitted. "We didn't really have anything like this where I'm from so it's just kind of... Strange." He trailed off. Emilia patted his back a couple of times to reassure him.

"If only you'd have seen the markets in Rosewood Creek." She laughed softly before taking the lead and having a wander around the different stalls. There were quite a few different vendors here, selling produce, wool and everything in between.

Emilia spotted a stall selling baked goods that had a small crochet fox near what looked like a tin box of change. She made her way over to it and couldn't resist picking out a couple of pastries for herself and Noah.

"Thank you," Emilia chirped politely as she passed over some change for the food. "We're not from around here, I don't suppose you know where we would be able to find the town of Havron?"

"Havron?" The woman double checked, prompting a nod from Emilia. "It's not that far actually, about half a days' ride West of here."

Emilia thanked her again, nudging Noah to get the map out and note it down just in case. They were about to leave, but the woman looked around the town centre anxiously before lowering her voice.

"I have to ask. Why do you need to go to Havron?" There was a shift in her tone of voice, it wasn't quite as friendly as before. Emilia noticed the change in body language, it felt more defensive now.

"I need to go get my friends. I've been told they're in Havron and I need to get to them as soon as possible. What do you know about the place?"

Emilia was preparing herself just in case she needed to defend herself, she didn't know if they were potentially in a spot of bother here.

"Are you with the rebellion?" The woman almost whispered, nervously, reaching for something nearby, though Emilia couldn't tell what. "Or are you with those... Whispers?"

"I am the Rebellion." Emilia whispered back without thinking her words through. Just the thought of being associated with the Whispers again made her feel sick.

A wave of relief washed over the woman and the tension in her shoulders dropped instantly. Emilia felt her own body relax as the woman let out a sigh of relief.

"Good." She laughed nervously. "Be careful though, they've taken over Havron. It's almost always got guards posted around, and they're armed. It's not safe anymore. If you left now it'll be well into the night when you get there. If you need somewhere to sleep tonight you are welcome in my home."

Emilia and Noah shared a glance, taking a moment to think about their next move.

"We could always get some rest and set off before sunlight, get there at a reasonable time. They'll know we'll be going so even if we turned up in the dead of night it still won't be a surprise." Emilia's words fell out quickly, almost as though she started speaking before even finishing the sentence in her head.

Noah nodded, thinking it through briefly.

"I think that's probably for the best, plus that way we'll be rested and ready for whatever they might throw at us."

In agreement, they graciously thanked the woman again for her hospitality and accepted the offer to rest in her home that evening.

What was left of the day seemed to pass at an excruciatingly slow pace. They tried to distract themselves by wandering through the town. They noticed a lot of orange weaved throughout the town. Some places they had visited in the past had the occasional supporter, but it was like the entire town was in favour of the revolution.

They discussed what might happen tomorrow, talked through different scenarios and how best to handle them should they arise. Neither of them knew what they would be walking into tomorrow, and they wanted to be as prepared as possible.

The woman kindly provided them with an evening meal, and Noah and Emilia insisted on cleaning up afterward to repay her kindness. Eventually they turned in for the night, though they both knew that they wouldn't be sleeping too long as they were both eager to try and get their friends back.

Thirty Seven

As informed, it did take the better part of the day to reach the town of Havron. It was just past midday when they saw a town come in to view. They didn't really know what they were looking for, but they just had to hope that they were heading in the right direction.

They were apprehensive, cautious as they got closer. Noah had informed Emilia of the many guards he had seen a lot sooner than her. As much as it was helpful, it made her nervous.

"Yeah, we are definitely walking right in to an ambush, aren't we?" Noah joked, trying his best to make light of the situation. Emilia just nodded, accepting the fate.

"We thought it could be, I don't mind going in alone if need be." Emilia suggested. Noah shook his head, tutting at the words coming out of her mouth.

"Don't be ridiculous. You know we stand a better chance together. We'll just have to take them all on." He joked, though he was most likely right. They were a lot stronger together, and if they did have to take on every single guard in this place, they would do it together.

They rode right up to the front gate where the guards were, there was no other way in - or out by the looks of things. One of the guards spoke into a radio, the words indistinguishable but she knew that people were being made aware of their arrival.

Swallowing the lump in her throat, they instructed them to dismount. They were stripped of their weapons and were let inside the town.

"I really don't like this." Emilia muttered to Noah as they walked inside. They had nothing, no horses, no weapons and neither of them knew if their powers would work inside the town - again, another thing they had discussed last night.

"We'll be ok." Noah tried to reassure her, giving her hand a light squeeze as they approached the middle of the town. It was a sandy coloured circle, the perimeter covered by guards. In the middle of the circle was the man Emilia despised the most. Vandona.

On one side of him, knelt down on the ground was Bailey. Hands were tied behind his back and he was covered in bruises and cuts. On the other side of Vandona was Connie, again on her knees with her wrists tied together behind her back. She was also covered in wounds.

Emilia did everything she could to keep herself calm. This had clear intention to aggravate her and she wanted to rise above that. They wanted to keep a safe distance between themselves and Alaric. They didn't know what was going to happen, so they didn't want to make any sudden moves or get too close right away, keeping themselves about ten metres away from him.

"Vandona." Emilia was the first to break the silence, her voice cutting through the air.

"Number thirty seven." He retorted, knowing just how much she hated being called that instead of her name. She bit her tongue, trying not to comment on it. She didn't want to give him the satisfaction.

"We've done this dance before, I think we can skip the pleasantries this time. What is it you want?" Emilia spoke firmly, sticking to the plan of Emilia doing the majority of the talking.

"You know what it is I want. I want the location of the gate!" His voice boomed across the barren landscape. "I want the power of the other realm, who knows what power it holds!"

The war that had been between Aglotar and Roanloch appeared to be long forgotten now, Alaric wanted more. He wanted power over an entirely new world instead of just this one.

"I don't know where the gate is, I've told you this before." Emilia reminded him, almost tired of this to and fro with him. Bailey looked up at Emilia with tired eyes, and she almost couldn't meet his gaze. Emilia left him behind. Not on purpose, of course, but seeing the results of her actions flooded her with guilt.

She managed to hold eye contact with him briefly, but as she did so she felt slightly confused. They weren't Bailey's eyes. She tried not to show it, but she also wanted to let Noah know, just without alerting anyone that she had started to catch on.

Looking over at Connie she saw something similar, it looked like her, but there were small details that gave it away - it wasn't them. It worried her, because if it wasn't Connie and Bailey, first of all, where were they? Second of all, who were the people in front of them?

The sound of a gunshot brought Emilia back to the present moment and she once again paid close attention to Alaric.

"Lies!" He shouted, slowly descending into madness. Power really did make people go crazy, and he hadn't even got it yet, who knows what kind of person he would be if he had it. "Lies! Lies! Lies! You know! You're the only one who has that... That impossible light! That's what the gate is made of! That godforsaken light!"

Instinctively, Emilia took a step back, he was acting like a maniac. Taking a breath and steadying her balance, she tried to think on her feet. Now was not the time for thinking because he pointed the gun at her. She wasn't scared of death, if it was meant to be it would have happened already.

"Since you're not cooperating, I'm going to give you a choice. Which one gets the bullet first?" He lowered his aim towards the two people on the ground just ahead of him.

"Lover boy Bailey?" He pointed the gun at the back of his head before switching sides and pointing it towards the female. "Or cute little Connie?"

"Stop this." Emilia said coldly. Alaric just laughed, changing his target every few seconds.

"If you're not going to help me and pick one, I'll have to choose one for you."

"Emilia." Noah's concerned voice came behind him, the worry clear in his voice. He still thought this was them, and they both knew that Alaric wasn't bluffing. He would gladly shoot one of them, he would have killed both of them already if he didn't need something. "Emilia we have to do something."

"Time's ticking, thirty seven. I'll give you to the count of ten. No no, that's too long. Five."

"Emilia?"

"Four."

"Stop this, Vandona."

"Three."

"Emilia, what's the plan?"

"Two."

"Vandona I am warning you. Let them go."

"Ooh, a threat." He laughed in a sing-song voice. "Some one's going to die."

"Emilia! Do something!"

"One."

"That's enough!" Emilia raised her hands and slowed time down, just for a few seconds, but it was enough to stop Alaric in his tracks. He stared her down, his eyes dark with excitement. "No one is dying here. First of all, that isn't Connie or Bailey. I don't know who they are but it's not them, so this little game isn't going to work on me."

"The time manipulation is new." Vandona smirked, who knows what he was thinking as he took in the newfound information. His demeanour changed once again. Back to the chirpy, crazy tone as before. "Well, if the shows over and you figured out it's not them, I suppose it doesn't really matter which one I kill then, does it?"

Within a second he shot the gun towards whichever target was closer to him, but Emilia had already anticipated his next move and had raised another hand at the same time he did in order to disarm him, his gun now on the floor away from him.

"I must not have made myself clear enough. I said no one here is dying." Emilia stated coldly. "When did I say their lives didn't matter?"

The harshness of her words had caused shock within everyone there. Blue light shrouded her, encased her even. She was channeling it in an impossible way that she hadn't shown before.

"You don't have them. You don't have Bailey, or Connie, or anyone. You're out of options, Vandona. You have nothing."

Emilia didn't know if he did or did not, she was just trying to make him sound weak. All she could do was hope that everyone she cared about was safe. Alaric started to laugh again. Emilia tried to hide her confusion.

"See, that's where you're wrong, Emilia. I have so much power and influence. So much more than you can even imagine." He clapped his hands together, which was shortly followed by a loud bell. A bell she recognised the tone of.

The guards that marked the perimeter all sprung into action at the sound of that bell.

Emilia could see arrows flying through the air towards them, so she grasped Noah's hand and sprinted towards the two people on the floor, shrouding them all in a blue hue, shielding them from the arrows.

"Onyx!" She called out, following the shout with a loud whistle. They had to get out of there. Yes, she was strong, but there was a lot of guards here, too many for them to take on right now. Their main priority was to get out of here.

The black mare raced in, and just as she had hoped, had her dagger. At least they had something. Emilia quickly cut the rope that bound the two unfortunate people on the floor, who had changed back to their usual form by the look of things.

"You have two options, either run. And I mean run, as fast as you can run and get the hell away from here, or you can come with us. But you need to make a decision right now, okay? Are you coming?" The two of them nodded eagerly, clearly happy to go with Emilia and Noah.

Noah, once in possession of his bow again was able to take down an impressive number of guards as they escaped Havron on horseback, the two new additions clinging on tightly as not to fall.

Emilia wasn't sure what the plan was after this, but she just knew she had to get everyone to safety first, then together they can try and come up with a plan.

Thirty Eight

Everyone was breathing heavily when they finally came to a stop. Adrenaline was pumping through Emilia's veins. Where they were she had no idea, nor had she noted just how long they had been riding for or in which direction they had headed.

The sky had darkened, filled with grey clouds that threatened rain, a storm was definitely on its way. Finding shelter was Emilia's first thought. She scanned the world around her, trying to weigh out her options. There was a vast expanse of forest in the distance, it would hide them well so long as they could make it there before the weather turned.

Despite Emilia wanting to try and find her close friends as soon as she could, she now had two more people that she felt responsible for, that she needed to keep safe while they were with her and Noah. The other option was to try and find a town nearby, which would be good for shelter and food, but it was often a risk as they never knew if the townsfolk would be on the rebel's side or if Alaric still had influence over them.

"There's a storm coming." Noah's voice brought her back to the present moment, she nodded in acknowledgement. "What do you want to do, Emilia?"

"I think the safest option is to head for that forest just west of here, it's big and there will likely be plenty of sheltered areas in there, and with any luck very few of Alaric's soldiers." She stated calmly before turning to the new recruits. "Welcome, by the way. My name is Emilia, this is Noah. You're free to leave if you'd like, but you're more than welcome to stick with us until you feel ready to go."

It was the first time Emilia had gotten a proper look at them since they escaped. The were thin, like they hadn't eaten properly in quite some time. She remembered the way she looked when she first escaped the facility she spent a year in, she had also lost a considerable amount of weight over her time in there.

They looked alike, so Emilia assumed they were siblings. A small age gap between them, too. The younger of them was a girl, long hair in a light, mousey shade of brown. The elder one only looked a few years older if that, his hair a similar shade of brown but cut quite short.

"My name is Eli," He spoke for both of them after a moment's hesitation, like they were trying to decide if they trusted the two strangers in front of them. Emilia had been in that position more times than she could count now. "This is my little sister Riley."

After a brief introduction, the siblings decided they were more than happy to stay with Emilia and Noah for the time being. They didn't know where they were, and they appeared to be quite weak and tired. The bruises only told part of the story, and she didn't need to imagine what horrors they may have been through.

Emilia rode with Riley, and Noah with Eli as they made their way towards the distant forest. Emilia didn't know those woods, but she felt safer in an environment like that than out in the open, where they would be exposed.

As expected, the rain started to fall before they had found shelter. Once in the forest, Emilia followed a small creek upstream until she found the source, and along with it a more rocky terrain. It didn't take long for them to find a small cave, it was cozy, but at least they would be out of the rain.

Emilia built a fire just inside the mouth of the cave while Noah went to acquire something to eat for the evening. Thankfully it wasn't too long until his safe return, because the rain was gradually getting worse. Noah had managed to catch not one, but two rather large hares. The rain made it a little easier on the hunt as it masked the sound of Noah's footsteps.

"You two try and get some sleep okay, I reckon we've got a long day tomorrow." Emilia told the siblings, who looked as though they were already starting to fall asleep now that their bellies were fuller.

"How did you know?" Noah asked quietly once the two siblings were fast asleep. "How did you know it wasn't Bailey?"

"The eyes." Emilia said softly. "Their eyes were different, a very minuscule detail, but it was there. I don't know if he's had them or not, but if he's using shapeshifter's as decoys, either he doesn't have them, or they're already dead. All we can do is hope."

Noah put an arm around her in a side hug as they sat together at the mouth of the cave, watching the storm from the dry interior. Emilia leant into him, smiling softly.

"I don't know where to go now." She admitted in a low voice. "I need to find them, but I just don't know where to even start looking. Havron was the only lead I had."

"We'll figure it out." Noah tried to ease her worries. "We'll just go town by town, seek out anyone who supports the revolution and go from there, see if they have seen Bailey, or have any information on him. Once we get him back-"

"I need to find Amana." Emilia interrupted. "I agree we need to get Bailey back, but Amana is so young, and if they discover her abilities, well, you heard Meladia, they can get through to the other realms. If that gate open all those shadow creatures will take over. Finding her is our top priority."

"Okay." Noah complied. "That's what we'll do, we'll keep looking for her and find her as soon as we can. Hopefully Alaric doesn't realise what he's let go of. He's so focussed on you that no one else seems to matter anymore."

Emilia nodded, Noah was right there. Every single weakness that he knew of, Alaric was trying to take advantage of. Leading her into traps with the hope that her friends are there. She didn't really want to let him get away as easy as he did, but she had people to protect.

Hopefully, they would be able to find somewhere safe for Eli and Riley to go, it was too dangerous for them to stay with Emilia for too long.

Noah and Emilia took turns throughout the night, one would sleep while the other kept watch until they couldn't do it any longer and swapping over. It worked quite well and by morning they both felt rested enough to start the long day ahead of them.

Thirty Nine

It didn't take too long to come across a small town after they left the safety of the forest. Sadly, no one had seen Amana, Bailey or any of the others they were in search of. Unfortunately, they had the same luck in the next few towns they visited.

The only positive that they had was that they were able to update their map accordingly, and even managed to get a hold of a more in-depth map of this part of Roanloch. It had cost them a bit of gold, but it was worth it because it helped then check off which towns they had already been to, which ones were supporting the revolution and which were against.

The majority they had visited were in favour of the revolution, thankfully. The numbers appeared to be shifting in favour of the revolution, perhaps one day they would be able to overthrow Alaric and take back the land properly. One day, perhaps, everyone would be able to live freely again, without fear. The way life should be.

They were on route to another town, just a little bit further south when they were stopped in their tracks by a figure in a dark brown cloak. Emilia was almost in tears as she immediately recognised who it was.

"Lorenzo!" She gasped, dismounting from Onyx and pulling him into a hug. "Oh my goodness, how good it is to see you!"

"Emilia, you're alive!" He beamed as he squeezed her tightly, excited to see her. "Gracie and I have been looking everywhere for you!"

Emilia felt her heart skip a beat as she realised that Gracie had found Lorenzo, but she didn't want to get her hopes up too high just yet.

"Amana... Is she?"

"Amana is doing so great, but she keeps asking about you." Lorenzo confirmed and Emilia pulled him into another hug.

"Thank you. I can't thank you or Gracie enough for keeping her safe!"

"Of course, it's the least we could do. You freed us. All of us. You need to come with me, it's... Honestly I don't have the words for it, you just need to come and see for yourself!"

The group followed Lorenzo, unsure of where exactly he was leading them. Eventually, a small settlement started to come in to view. It was an unmarked town on the map, one that they had started to build up themselves. Emilia was in awe as they got closer. Everyone was working together, using their powers to help each other.

People with exceptional strength were helping to move large blocks of stone made by those with earth based abilities, forming buildings. There was a well in the middle of it all that was constantly filled with water, courtesy of those with water based abilities.

Emilia looked around in disbelief, she couldn't believe what they had accomplished. It was something to truly be proud of. It felt like home, in all the best possible ways.

"There you are, stranger." Came a familiar voice. She swiftly turned around to see Bailey, no current bruises or injuries. Alive and well. Emilia rushed into his arms, pulling him into a tight hug, she couldn't deny she was ecstatic to see him. He wrapped his arms around her in return. "You alright, Em?"

"Yeah, it's just been a rough week. I'm glad to see you're doing okay." She admitted as she reluctantly pulled away. "What is this place?"

"We haven't settled on a name yet, nothing seems to have stuck. It's a place for all of us to be ourselves, a safe haven, an asylum for anyone with abilities that needs somewhere to go." Bailey explained, a proud look on his face.

"You did this?" Emilia asked inquisitively.

"Not just me, I helped start it and it just started to grow over the last week after the battle up North. We'd been building up the rebellion before we took on the facility that you were in, trying to grow in numbers. Of course we lost a lot of good people that day, but afterwards we all decided we needed a place to recover and rest. We found a place to call home for now, and we're starting to get somewhere now."

Emilia took in his words, recalling the day from her own memories, but more than that she remembered the bodies that were still there, yet to be buried or moved. It was heartbreaking, really. She noticed Bailey looking around, a look of confusion on his face.

"Is Taylor not with you?"

Emilia's face dropped, sadness overcoming her once again and she shook her head slowly.

"Taylor... She didn't make it. Alaric made sure of that." Emilia said in a low tone.

"Oh." Bailey said solemnly as the realisation hit. He tried to swallow the lump in his throat as he looked over to where Noah was speaking to some younger people that Bailey didn't recognise. "I see."

"Yeah." She sighed. "She's home, though. We buried her at home, where she belongs."

"Home?" Bailey asked with a raised eyebrow.

"Home." Emilia reiterated with a soft smile. "I still don't know how it happened, but we were lead back to Rosewood Creek. She's buried near our favourite lookout point, overlooking the lake. It's nice."

"How's Noah doing?" Bailey asked cautiously, his eyes again finding him across the little town.

"Not great, you know. He's lost the love of his life, it's not easy." Emilia spoke truthfully, knowing how hard Noah was trying to keep spirits up and keep going despite everything.

"I'll go speak with him, I know you have someone else that wants to see you." He smiled fondly, giving her another brief hug before making his way over to Noah.

Emilia, wandered further into the town, but didn't make it far before she was tackled with a hug from a very excited Gracie.

"Emmy!" She squealed, even jumping up and down a little kid when she was out of the hug. "I can't believe you actually blew it all up! Ahh! I mean I know you said that's what you were going to do, but I didn't think you'd actually do it!"

The teenager excitedly chatted away, almost as though Emilia had never been separated from her. It started to become white noise to her until she felt her grab her hand.

"Come on, I'll take you to see Amana!"

Gracie led Emilia to a little hut, with spaces for windows but no glass. The inside was small, a few tables and chairs and a whiteboard up at the front. They'd made a little classroom. It almost felt like life was back to normal.

"Bailey insisted on it. One of the first things he set up. Said education was important." Gracie stated, almost letting out a little giggle. "You wait here, I'm going to bring Amana out!"

Emilia wasn't given a say in this decision, and before she could object Gracie had already gone inside. For some reason it made her nervous, the last time she saw Amana, Emilia had promised her she would meet them just outside, by the river. A promise that she broke unintentionally, though it still plagued her with guilt.

Moments passed and before Emilia could get lost in her own worry, the door burst open, and Amana rushed into Emilia, small hands gripping tightly onto her. Tears formed in the outer creases of her eyes. Emilia held Amana just as close, if not more so.

This place was almost perfect. Her loved ones were safe, creating a haven for people of all different walks of life. There was just one person missing from it; Connie.

Forty

Walking through the small settlement that they had made, Emilia felt at home. There was joyful chatter in the air and spirits were high. All around her, there were people practicing their powers with one another.

It almost reminded her of the days she spent in the facility, but it was completely different now. People were training willingly, and there was laughter from both sides as they took turns learning their strengths, weaknesses and everything in between.

The way it should have always been, really. They all came together as a community; they tended to the community garden, and they had even acquired some livestock already, potentially from nearby towns. There were people teaching others life skills like fishing, first aid, foraging. It warmed her heart. It made her feel as though everything they had done up until this point, was finally worth it.

Emilia didn't want to scare them with everything she had recently learned, though she did need to speak with Bailey about it. After all, Emilia still had a job to do and she needed to ensure that she kept her world, and her family, safe.

"Okay," Bailey said, taking in everything Emilia had told him about. From the shadow creatures, to the gate, to Amana potentially being the one who can open it. "Well, Amana is safe with us, so surely nothing more will come of it, right?"

"I don't know, Bailey." Emilia admitted, rubbing her arm nervously. "It's serious. From what Meladia has told us, this could be detrimental not just to our world, but to every single realm there is. We were given our gifts for a reason, and we have to do what's right. We can't just sit about and wait on the off chance it doesn't happen, we have to make sure it can never happen. We have to take down Alaric and destroy the gate."

"You know that's no easy feat, Emilia. I tried taking down his base in Havron with a good bunch from here, we barely escaped with our lives." Bailey countered. "It's just not worth it. He has too much power, we spent the better part of a year infiltrating his smaller facilities and that was hard enough. How many more lives do you want to lose?"

"None!" Emilia raised her voice slightly, mildly infuriated by his tone. "I'm trying to save as many people as I possibly can. I can only do so much alone, Bailey. I need you. I need as many people behind me as we can manage, the revolution is spreading more than you know, but people are scared. If we don't lead by example none of us will ever be safe. No one will ever be free."

Noah cleared his throat, interrupting Bailey and Emilia's debate before it got too heated. Neither of them were known for backing down. Their stubbornness, on the other hand, was a well known fact at this point. Both of them turned their heads towards him, awaiting what he had to say.

"I think Bailey needs to hear from Meladia himself. The gravity of the situation isn't sinking in just from your words, Emilia." Both of them opened their mouths to start to protest, but Noah raised his hands. "Nothing against either of you, you both make completely valid points. You forget though, that Meladia isn't of this world, and therefore has limited emotional attachments to it. Meaning that she is the most qualified to give as neutral opinion on what is necessary for the benefit of everyone."

His words lingered in the air and glances were exchanged between the three adults. Bailey pursed his mouth shut, he looked as though he was holding back another argumentative comment.

"Fine." Bailey reluctantly agreed. "We can leave at first light, maybe enjoy one night of freedom, Emilia. You've earned it, not every moment of living has to be a fight for survival."

Emilia was taken aback by his stark statement, and she stayed silent, watching as Bailey turned his back and walked away.

"Well, that went well." Noah said sarcastically, looking over at Emilia's confused look. "I still think it's the best idea though, maybe the reality of everything will sink in after he meets Meladia. I know I felt different."

"Thanks, Noah." Emilia smiled, patting his arm in thanks. A small gesture, but a meaningful one none the less. Over the last week the two of them had started to build a close bond between each other. "I hope so, there's still so much to lose."

* * *

How does one enjoy a night of freedom when the weight of who knows how many worlds rest on your shoulders? Emilia bounced her leg restlessly as she watched the flicker of the fire in front of her.

Noah handed her a cup of something, she wasn't sure what but she drank it regardless. It was a little bitter, but also had a citrus like aftertaste. It eased the constant worry residing in her head, if only a little bit.

There was music coming from nearby, rhythmic drumming accompanied with a small stringed instrument. It was a folksy tune, light in tone and lifting people's spirits. Before long, words were added to the shanty.

We have to be strong,

> *We have to be fast,*
> *We know how to run,*
> *We know how to outlast.*

Her leg stopped it's bouncing sporadically, instead tapping along to the steady beat as she closed her eyes, trying to take in the evening in for what it was; a lovely night.

> *Some will turn away,*
> *They hang their heads low,*
> *They say ignorance is bliss,*
> *And they pretend that they don't know.*

As the first verse was sung again, more voices started to join in. After all, everyone had been through a lot. They deserved to enjoy a night by the fire, singing and drinking.

> *Some will turn you in,*
> *They don't care who you are,*
> *They say money is a killer,*
> *But it never gets you far.*

Emilia wasn't sure when, but Noah had replenished her drink again. A warmth was slowly flowing through her, the alcohol slowly taking an affect on her.

Everyone once again joined in during the repeated chorus.

> *We'll change our future, change our fate*
> *From the past we all will flee,*
> *Learn from our mistakes,*
> *And one day we'll be free.*

There was food plentiful that people helped themselves to. They were a growing community, but the way they all shared everything was something Emilia had merely dreamed of for years, the name of this place was not decided, but already it felt as much a home to her as Rosewood Creek did. She found herself singing along with those around her by the time the song concluded, something inside her healing ever so slightly.

The blissful feeling couldn't last forever, and even though the joyful gathering continued on, Emilia slinked away from it, finding herself on the edge of the village, letting herself get lost a little in her own thoughts. She scaled the watch tower the town had built and made it all the way up to the top, the brisk night air causing goosebumps to form along her arms. She laid back, looking up at the starry expanse above her, longing, wishing for everything to be okay.

Bailey had watched her walk away from the centre of the village, and couldn't help but roll his eyes as he saw her climb the watchtower.

"The girl doesn't know how to even take one night off." He scoffed aloud to those around him, gesturing his hands in the direction in which she went. Noah was one of the ones that heard his comment. His mouth curled slightly upwards at one side in a slight smile, he knew Bailey wasn't saying it maliciously, despite his tone.

Noah knew, that Bailey cared in his own way, still, he felt a need to defend Emilia. It appeared that Bailey needed a reminder of everything she had been through, and Noah had been waiting for a moment to set the record straight, so when Bailey had stepped away from the crowd of people, Noah took the opportunity to pull him aside and say his piece.

"Cut her a bit of slack, Bay." He said gently, taking a drink of the liquid in his cup. "She might be on the edge a little, but you've got to think, in the last few weeks she's kind of been through it; she jumped into the back of a van she knew was headed somewhere she would likely be powerless, swiftly blew it up sometime afterwards, all without our help, her best friend was killed right in front of her, whom she then had to bury, to then learn that she is one of the only ones who can stop the world from being destroyed."

Bailey was silent, staring down at his own drink in shame, though it didn't stop Noah.

"Even then, she didn't even stop to mourn, she started looking for you; for Amana. We've even been to Havron. Alaric used shapeshifters that looked like you and Connie to try and get her to cooperate but even then she held her nerve. Even I was panicking, he was going to shoot them there was no doubt about that. I know you've been through a lot yourself, and you've built this place from the ground up while she's been gone, but just give her time."

Bailey barely managed to look Noah in the eyes after he had finished speaking, biting his lip in hesitation, as though he was trying to stop the next words coming out of his mouth.

"She left us behind, Noah. She left us to fight off the rest of those soldiers in the vans. She's stronger than all of us combined, we got lucky that they stopped engaging once they managed to put enough distance between us and them!" Bailey snapped a little. "She's reckless, she doesn't think her actions through. Even when we managed to track her down what does she do? She blew it all up. There might have been information in there that we could use against them! She might have taken you with her, but she left me behind. She got you out of there and left me in the middle of that battleground. I could have died and none of you would've even known."

"Feel a bit better now?" Noah questioned, taking in Bailey's body language and how his chest was rising and falling at a more rapid pace than usual. He smiled at his friend, knowing he must have felt so much better now he had said his piece. After all, it was healthy to clear the air. "It's good to get it off your chest, no use in bottling it up."

Noah patted Bailey on the back in comfort before he stood up and stretched, announcing that he was going to turn in for the night, suggesting Bailey do the same as they were setting off at first light, quoting his words from earlier on in the day. He turned back after a few steps to get one final word in.

"Oh, and Bailey, for the record, she feels awful about leaving you behind she really does, but in her defence, she was unconscious."

Forty One

Emilia felt the warmth from the sun on her face even before she fully awoke, embracing the first rays of the day. Stretching her limbs out, she turned over in her half-asleep state, her arm drooping off the side of the watchtower roof.

"Wakey wakey, Warren." Noah called up to her from the bottom of the tower. "No sudden moves though, can't have you breaking any bones before you save the world."

Slowly, Emilia opened her eyes, quickly realising that she was on the very edge, swiftly moving back towards the middle before making her way down.

"You do know they have beds here, right? Like actual beds, if you remember what they are." Noah teased her, watching as she rubbed the back of her stiff neck, trying to shake off the uncomfortable sleeping position.

"I remember what a bed is." She bashfully retorted, unable to think of a witty comeback in her half-asleep state. "Everyone else ready to go?"

Noah shrugged.

"Only as ready as you are, I'm sure it won't take long till we're on the road to Rosewood again." He reassured.

Emilia nodded, while stifling a yawn.

"Meet back here in ten?" She suggested, and upon agreement she set off to gather her belongings and find Amana - she was very eager to make sure she wasn't separated from her again. Noah had helped Eli and Riley get settled in to the village when they arrived, but she made sure to check up on then before she left.

Emilia also made a point to go and see Gracie and Lorenzo before she left, after all she still didn't know what the plan would be after they paid a visit to Meladia. She thanked them again for watching over Amana when she couldn't. Everything they did she was appreciative of, and couldn't thank them enough.

The minutes flew by and she made her way back to the watchtower. Noah and Bailey were already there, ready to go, just waiting on her.

The journey was much shorter this time around, it was a lot easier when you had a proper map to help you chart your way across the lands. Even without it they would have been fine, Emilia was much more familiar with the land now that she had been home longer. She led the way with the confidence of a leader.

Whilst it was a sight that Emilia and Noah were sadly familiar with, Bailey started to slow down when they entered Rosewood Creek, taking in the ruins around him with saddened eyes. He had heard Emilia speak so fondly of this place over the years, and he had imagined it so full of life as she had described in detail time and time again. It almost felt as though he was seeing his own home in ruin.

As the small group entered the forest, they could feel the shift in the air; even the atmosphere surrounding Meladia had a magical aura. Emilia led them to the waterfall, where she could feel Meladia's presence the strongest.

Moments passed and there was a quiet rustling, the wind changing, and slowly Meladia appeared in front of them. Emilia smiled, it was just like seeing an old friend for her now. Even Noah felt more comfortable in her presence this time.

Bailey, on the other hand, was stunned. Granted, Emilia had told him about the spirit, but to see her with his own eyes was something else entirely. It was awe-inspiring.

"What brings you back quite so soon, Emilia?" The spirit spoke in her soft, elegant tone. She let out a soft gasp as she laid eyes on Amana, kneeling down before her. "Why hello, sweetheart. If I'm not mistaken, you must be Amana. I've heard so much about you."

Amana couldn't hide the grin from her face, she was also awestruck from the sight of the spirit before her and all she managed to do was nod and give a shy wave. Meladia rose from the ground to face Bailey, giving him a soft smile.

"It's nice to finally meet you, Mr Larson. You've made quite the impact across Ebratha."

"I erm-" Bailey cleared his throat, trying to find his words. "Thank you. I think."

"Of course." Meladia let out a light giggle, trying to ease his nerves before . "A positive impact, Bailey. You've come a long way from where you started, my lovely."

A small, but proud smile started to form on his face. He still wasn't completely used to words of affirmation, but he was slowly improving at accepting them. Emilia spoke up from the side of him.

"The Nox Malum, Meladia." She started, a little unsure. "What exactly are we up against with them? What do we need to do?"

Meladia's smile faltered, a more serious look across her face. She saw the way Emilia's eyes shifted over to where Bailey was standing, a noticeable tension in the air. Meladia dramatically raised her arms, using what power she still retained to make the world around them shift. The colours started to drain right before their eyes.

"The Nox Malum are relentless creatures that will destroy anything and everything we hold dear." The scenery around them, the trees and flowers wilted and shrivelled up until they were nothing but dust. "They do not stop until they have absorbed everything in their path, ever hungry for more and reducing everything in their way to nothing more than dust and rubble. Sometimes not even that."

Gracefully conducting her arms in a circular motion around her, the damage started to reverse.

"A long, long time ago, myself and my brothers and sisters were able to repel them. We sanctioned them off, creating a new realm entirely made of darkness, in hopes it would starve the creatures of nourishment and we prayed that the exile would destroy them."

She used her blue light to draw the outline of an arch, a gateway.

"We sealed them off in that realm and we hoped, we prayed that would be the end of it, that our actions were final and life would continue as it once did before."

Around them, the surroundings began to return to how they were before Meladia's theatrical explanation.

"We agreed that the best way to prevent it happening again would be to each reside in a realm and keep it safe for the rest of eternity. We are protectors. It is what we do. There comes a time where the title is passed forward, to another soul that is just and deserving."

Meladia gestured to Emilia, who was not expecting to have the spotlight on her in that moment.

"There was only one that I could entrust with such a delicate, yet heavy, responsibility. And that is Emilia." She walked towards the young woman, taking her hands in her own. "You are the one that needs to strengthen the veil between worlds. For years you have been growing stronger, but as have the Nox Malum. I'm afraid the time has come, it can't wait any longer, I fear the worst will become true if left unattended much longer."

"But how? I don't know what to do or how to do it." Emilia admitted quietly, as though trying to keep it a secret from the others around them.

"I can help you find the weakest spot. That is something I can help you with. You need to go to it, and force back the darkness within with everything you have. Your light will guide you and everything will fall in to place."

"You said we need the gatekeeper, too. What part in that do they play?" Emilia asked hesitantly, choosing her words carefully as she had yet to talk in depth about this with Amana. She didn't want to scare the young girl too much before it was necessary.

"Why of course, they will create the pathway for you to break through and breach the gap between realms." Meladia responded as though it was common knowledge. "Just as you will know what to do when the time comes, as will they."

"Emmy," Came the small, timid voice of Amana, which surprised everyone around them. She gestured for Emilia to move in closer, and whispered in her ear. "I can open the gate for you."

The silence in the air around them after the whispered words was eerie. Emilia had expected to sit Amana aside and carefully explain it all to her, along with the risks of what it entailed. She had been dreading the conversation, but as soon as it appeared to have begun it was over.

"You... You know you're the gatekeeper?" Emilia asked her cautiously. "How long have you known?"

"A while." Amana nervously clasped her hands together, fiddling with them, her voice in a quiet tone. "I'm sorry. I didn't know. Everyone had powers, I didn't know mine were that special. I use them mostly for getting away from scary places. I couldn't do it in the van or in that bad place we were in before, but I don't know why. The light that Miss Meladia just made with that archway is what it looks like when I do it, too."

Emilia couldn't help but pull the young girl in to a hug. The things she must have been through for her to discover she had a way of escaping when she needed to, Emilia did her best not to think too much into it.

"I know it's a lot to ask of you, Amana, and it's going to be dangerous."

"That's okay, Emmy. I can do it. I know I can."

The young girl tried to sound confident in herself, but everyone could hear how unsure and how nervous she was. Bailey didn't look pleased at the situation. Given his past, Emilia could understand why he would be against them needing to use Amana's powers. He just wanted her to be able to be a child, learn in school and make friends her own age. Instead, this was what she needed to do.

"Okay, great. The kid's happy to help." Bailey stated, his face stoic and his tone flat. "How do we find where this gate is?"

It was a valid question, as Emilia herself wasn't sure on how to answer him. She looked over to Meladia for help.

"Emilia, Amana." Her soft voice called over. "Come with me."

They followed the spirit, and she lead them to a big open space. The clearing that Emilia was very familiar with. Gently, Meladia took their hands and encouraged them to take a deep breath and close their eyes.

"You both have a connection to the gate, somewhere deep inside you, you know where it is. Together, you need to find it." There was a brief pause, and Emilia went to open her mouth. "No questions, Emilia. Just follow your light."

Amana let out a quiet giggle at the comment, keeping her own eyes closed, holding on to the others.

A few moments passed, all three of them quiet as they searched. Amana let out a soft gasp.

"I see it." She exclaimed, keeping her eyes closed all the while. It wasn't long until Emilia could see the destination, too.

Together, they all focussed their energies on the location of the gate, trying to pinpoint it's exact location.

Suddenly, a flash of light burst out from them, and it shot up into the sky, like it was also searching. It flew up and out of sight until it found it's target. The light was a beacon in the sky, showing them where they needed to be. Now all they had to do was to follow it.

"Who else can see that, Meladia?" She asked hesitantly, worried about who else would be able to see the location of the gate.

"No one. Just us. Not even Noah or Bailey will be able to see that beam." The spirit reassured her. "I wish you both the very best of luck."

Forty Two

The journey was long, the beam had taken them away from Roanloch once more, back to the heart of Aglotar. Their group had grown, however, as both Lorenzo and Gracie had been adamant on joining them, on helping them wherever they could. They had briefly returned to the growing settlement to stock up on supplies for the journey, and the teenagers wouldn't let them leave without them.

Emilia was thankful for it, and she appreciated how much they had both matured since the last time she saw them, it as easy to forget that at the end of the day they were still kids, but they didn't give the group a say and demanded they joined.

The Gracie she knew before would have bolted at the first chance and never looked back, yet here she was, riding into danger alongside her.

Everyone knew the risks that they were taking, and they knew exactly what was at stake, Emilia owed it to them to tell them the truth about what they were going to be up against, a part of her was hoping it would deter them so they would stay back, after all she did worry for their safety. It had done nothing but make the duo even more determined than before.

* * *

The sun was starting to set, and they were just trying to find somewhere to set up camp for the evening. Time was of the essence, of course, and Emilia longed to just keep going, but she knew they must rest. They needed their strength and if she kept pushing everyone, they wouldn't even make it to the beam before they passed out from exhaustion.

Noah had seen a small spot up ahead, just off the trail they were currently on. Everyone has happy to trust his judgement and let him lead the way. It was a small clearing, just past the tree line, plenty of cover to hide them from view should they need it.

They were efficient by now, they had been travelling together for quite some time now as the venture back into the heart of Aglotar had taken them a good month and then some. Before long they had a nice little fire going, ready to cook up whatever Noah was able to hunt.

The woodlands weren't as lush as they were back in Roanloch, and the wildlife wasn't as much in abundance here, but they made do. Emilia and Bailey had mastered the art of creating traps too, which they would set up so they had something ready to give them energy for the early mornings.

As usual, Emilia had volunteered to take first watch, and to her surprise, Bailey had offered to join her. Not wanting to cause a scene or make a fuss, she let him.

They still hadn't talked much since their disagreement, but they still worked well together regardless.

It didn't take long for everyone to drift off into a slumber, breathing was deep and there was the occasional snore, it was almost relaxing. Up until Bailey cleared his throat.

"I just wanted to apologise." He started off, trying to choose his words wisely. "I was harsh and out of line before. I didn't know how serious everything was. I'm sorry."

"I'm sorry, too." Emilia spoke softly, her words just above a whisper. "I'm sorry I hurt you, and I'm sorry I didn't tell you sooner. Everything has been so crazy lately I can barely keep up." She admitted quietly.

Bailey's body visibly relaxed, the tension slowly falling away. Though hesitant at first, he wrapped an arm around her shoulder, embracing her from the side. His muscles seemed to relax ever further as Emilia smiled and leant into him.

"We're only about a day's travel away from Dalmaroi now, you know." Bailey said quietly. "You doing okay?"

Emilia looked up into the night sky, up towards the beam of light. It was so close now, they didn't have much further to go. Meladia had insisted that Emilia would know what to do in due time, but she still didn't know what to expect. In the morning they would need to come up with a plan of action, so they were all on the same page and knew what to do should they be separated.

"I'm not sure. I'll let you know when it's all over." Emilia managed a small smile, despite the uncertainty that flooded her mind.

The snap of a twig on the ground brought Emilia out from her thoughts, her body tense.

"Relax, it was probably just a squirrel or something." Bailey said quietly, but Emilia disagreed. She rose to her feet, ready for a fight if necessary.

"My people have you surrounded." Came a very familiar voice, that Emilia never expected to hear again. "And they're very excited to see you."

The light from the fire lit up her face as she stepped forward again, Emilia racing forward to bring her into a tight embrace.

"It's good to see you again, Emilia."

"I thought you were dead." Emilia managed to choke out, trying to keep the tears back. After a moment she pulled herself away, her face damp despite how hard she tried to fight it. "Connie... Don't you dare scare me like that again!"

It wasn't long before the others made themselves known, Myla was there, as was Jep, and a few others that Emilia recognised from Gold Dust Grove. The commotion had woken the others up, and introductions were passed around, as well as a brief explanation as to what had been happening in Aglotar.

Connie had been growing her own band of rebels in Aglotar even after Emilia and Bailey had left, the tables were turning and the revolution was almost at tipping point. Alaric still had the upper hand with his wealth and power, but the scales were almost evenly balanced.

Alaric had gone above everybody now, and both sides of the split were united with a common enemy, one that they had to take down together in order to bring peace back to their lands. It appeared that Connie's rebels had also been planning on taking down Alaric, they were just waiting for the right moment to strike.

Emilia shared the information they had about the gate, and what was at stake should they fail their mission to destroy it, and seal it off forever, locking away the Nox Malum.

"I saw you, you know." Emilia said quietly. "I saw them hitting you, you were bruised, nothing but skin and bones."

"I know." Connie said, her voice nervous. "I saw you, too, that screen went both ways. I've never seen you angry like that before. I don't know what you did but something completely cut off the power and you were gone. The guards near me couldn't get it back no matter how hard they tried. It was only a few days later when Jep managed to get me out, actually."

"I finally met Jep. I went back to Gold Dust as soon as I could, he told me everything that happened. I don't think he likes me very much."

"No, that's just the way he is." Connie laughed, "He told me you two had finally met the first time he broke in to one of them and saved me. I think I started getting on his nerves at one point but they're so good for information. It got to a point I was basically turning myself in to Alaric every few months!"

"Yeah, they are actually. I've been in a fair few of them myself, now." Emilia let out a breathy laugh. "I really am glad to see you, Connie."

"Me too, Emmy."

Emilia slept soundly when her watch was up, a feeling of security encasing her now that she knew Connie was alive, safe and well. She was surrounded by those she loved, and she felt more sure in herself, more confident now that she would be able to do what she needed to do.

In the morning, they would plan out their attack together, they were even stronger than before with the new additions to the group.

Forty Three

Connie was very familiar with the location that they were headed, and as expected, it was one of Alaric's bases. The biggest of all of them by the looks of it, even larger than the one the Censorship Agency resided in. Unfortunately, it was one that only one had ever set foot in. The only person that had ever came out of it alive; Matra, who Connie had recruited swiftly after his escape.

"I think the best plan of action is to draw them away from the gate. Create a distraction so big that they need all their men in one place." Bailey suggested as they looked down at the rough map of the area that they had drawn into to ground as they planned their approach, his eyes meeting Emilia's as he spoke.

"So that would be me, yes?" Emilia piped up, almost sarcastically. "We all know he's after me, but how do we make it such a big thing?"

"Why don't we get his attention by destroying some of the neighbouring buildings?" Gracie suggested, pointing out some buildings at the front of the drawing. "So you could be in the middle of them here, and we blow up these two surrounding you, that has to draw out some of their men at least."

"You've found a right little pyromaniac, Emilia." Myra chuckled. "But it could work."

"We could definitely help you with that, we have plenty of explosives that we've seized from their facilities." Connie confirmed. "And Gracie's right, it would likely get their attention, especially with you in the middle."

"You know it's going to be a tough battle, don't you?" Bailey spoke up softly, apprehensive. "And you will need to somehow break away so you can find the gate."

"That's where our little superstar comes in. Amana is small, she'll be able to sneak in through a different way." Emilia smiled over at her, before looking at Connie. "You said a lot of these had rather large ventilation systems, right?"

"Yes. Matra knows them well, and he can change form, too, so he will also be able to fit in the vents. I trust him so I know Amana will be safe with him. Once they have located the gate they will radio us the location and we can get Emilia to it. Bailey is the strongest and a fantastic fighter, so I think the safest option is for Emilia to go with him."

"You do know that I'm probably fine to go alone, right?" Emilia reminded them. Both Connie and Bailey shared a knowing glance.

"Yes, you are, but it's safer to at the very least go in a pair. We don't know what we're going to be up against, not exactly, anyways." Connie said, not wanting to cause offence. Emilia nodded in understanding after taking in her words.

Everyone agreed with the plan, and were happy to proceed with it. There was no failsafe, no plan b. They couldn't afford to think like that, they needed it to work the first time around, it was the only way they would have the element of surprise they needed to lure everyone out.

"I don't know how many will turn up, but I have sent word to the other rebels with the location, so there may be more people joining." Connie informed the group, looking back at Emilia. " You'd be surprised with how many people are willing to fight when it's something they believe in, and people believe in you, Emilia."

"They do? Why?" She asked confused, surprised by her words. Connie furrowed her brows, returning her look of confusion.

"Look at what you've done, Emilia. Look at what's come of it. There are people banding together, finding family and friends in those who have shared a similar experience. You started it all." Connie looked over towards Bailey. "And your story has also spread to the masses. About how you overcame the conditioning. It truly gave people hope. Something some of them haven't had in a long long time."

Bailey's lips twitched into a small smile, pride washing over him. Connie's words moving him, he had not realised people had spread tales about his past with the Whisper's, but now he was thankful for it.

"Thank you, Connie." Emilia spoke up for both of them. "But I think you deserve some credit, too. You welcomed me with open arms, just as you did for many others who needed help before me. You are just as much a part of this revolution as any of us."

"This is all very moving," Noah spoke up. "But we really need to get this mission underway."

Nodding, the group packed up - they needed to make a quick stop in a nearby encampment to retrieve the explosives needed for the plan, but once that was done they were to head straight into the belly of the beast and take on Alaric for once and for all.

* * *

Bailey was right, it was about a day's worth of travel to the capital city of Aglotar. Not wanting to get too close, and risk alerting Alaric of their presence, they decided to lay low in one of the run down buildings just on the outskirts of the city.

Dalmaroi really was a beautiful city, especially as the sun was going down. The tall buildings across the city were very futuristic; modern. The glass exterior of the structures made for a beautiful backdrop, the light reflecting on one, then another, and another.

Emilia had never seen the capital of Aglotar in person before. It was bittersweet, really, as they would be destroying some of the beautiful architecture come the morning. It had to be done, she reminded herself. It was for the wellbeing of everyone in Ebratha.

Resting came difficult, with adrenaline and anxieties rising amongst the group. They took watches in pairs, not wanting to take any chances of them being ambushed. Like Connie said before, it was safer to do things together.

Myla relieved Emilia of her duty at one point in the evening, but even then she struggled to sleep. So much could go wrong tomorrow, they could lose everyone, they might not even find the gate.

"It'll all be okay." Said a quiet voice. Amana. Emilia smiled at the reassurance from the little one. Amana cuddled in to Emilia, helping her feel more at ease. "We'll be alright."

Amana's voice put Emilia's mind at ease, and eventually, she succumbed to her tiredness.

Forty Four

Emilia looked up at the buildings as they approached. She was leading them into what would most likely be the most dangerous mission any of them had done. Amana and Matra had set off already, on route to what they assumed was their main building. The beam of light Emilia had been following had led them to it, and it was finally time to take action.

There were two pairs that had split from the group also, the ones that were planting explosives in the buildings, the explosives that would draw everyone out, right to Emilia.

A sense of peace encompassed her, one way or another, everything will be over come this days' end. With Connie on her left, and Bailey on her right she kept going. Myla and Jep were in the middle, with some of Connie's rebels that had joined. Noah, being the skilled archer he was, was bringing up the rear, it gave him a better vantage point, after all. If Selenite was anything like Onyx, Noah would likely be unstoppable in the midst of battle.

Radio chatter brought Emilia back to the present day, trying not to worry about her friends too much.

"They're ready." Bailey announced flatly, as he looked around at the group. His eyes landed on

Connie, as if asking her an unspoken question. She nodded, her face serious. Bailey returned the nod, before speaking into the radio. "All set to go on our side, over."

There was silence amongst the group as they waited with baited breath. The first building was ablaze seconds later, accompanied with a deafening bang. An alarm was quick to follow, Bailey's face tensed up at the sound of it. Everyone knew exactly what that meant.

Before long the second building was up in flames, the group striding through the centre of both of them. Gunfire filled the city, from all sides.

Emilia quickly realised that the explosions had also been a signal for any rebels waiting in the shadows to strike. People charged in on the city from all around, Connie had been right after all, people really were willing to fight.

* * *

Amana waited patiently, silently with her new friend, Matra. He was nice, he had family of his own, brothers and sisters that were also a part of the rebellion. Amana picked nervously at the skin around her nails as they continued to wait.

They had set off early to make sure they had a clear view of the way in they needed to take. There were guards everywhere, so they had to tread carefully and just wait for the signal.

"We're ready when you guys are, over." Came a voice from the radio. Matra had lowered the volume to a level where its was only just audible, they had to keep hidden until the distraction brought the guards away from their posts.

It didn't take long, and Amana flinched as the buildings were blown up. The smoke filling the sky above. Before long, the guards that were patrolling near their designated entrance left their post, just as they had hoped, heading in to battle.

The two of them moved quickly, breaking into the ventilation shaft and squeezing inside, Matra shrunk himself down into the form of a ferret while Amana replaced the vent grate, making it look untouched to help them stay as undetected as possible.

Matra was there to protect her should anything happen, but in this form he could also venture into different rooms quickly. He was fast and could assess any danger should there be any.

Together they manoeuvred through the large building. It wasn't too long before Amana felt something calling to her, pulling her in.

"We need to go down." She informed Matra. "It's not up here, it's somewhere down below."

Matra nodded, trying to find a way to descend through the vents. Eventually, they came to a drop down. Amana pushed her hands against both sides of the shaft and carefully let herself down, sinking lower and lower, with Matra carefully perched on her shoulders.

It felt as though it went on forever, but eventually they reached the bottom. They moved along, passing several rooms, Amana leading the way. She could feel the presence of the other worlds, they were close. She passed another room, but had to double back.

"In there." She whispered to Matra, who quickly exited the vents to scout the room. He returned after a moment or two, back in his human form.

"Empty. No one down here at all, I don't think." He reassured Amana, who crawled out afterwards. "But there's no gate here, either." His voice was filled with concern, maybe even doubt. Amana shook her head.

"We can't see it, but it's there. I know it is. I can feel it. We need to let Emilia know."

Matra nodded, trusting her words. He pulled the radio out of the bag Amana had been carrying, and informed Bailey of their position.

* * *

"Copy that, we're on the way, over." Bailey spoke into the radio after repeating the location back to them, just to be sure. He put his fingers to his mouth and let out an ear-piercing whistle to get Emilia's attention.

With dagger in hand, Emilia finished off the guard she was in combat in, looking back over to Bailey at the sound of the signal. Amana had found the gate. She looked over to Connie, who was in the thick of a fight herself, but she caught Emilia's eye and nodded. Silently wishing her the best of luck.

There were bodies all around them, whether they were with Alaric or Emilia, it didn't matter anymore. Emilia just wanted this to be over. Hopefully, if she could close the gate, everything would come to a halt. The endless and meaningless fighting would cease and there would finally be peace. She thought back to Meladia, how the evil that the Nox Malum bring can seep in to the realms through the tiniest of cracks. It could be the reason that Alaric is the way he is. Or maybe he himself was just another form of evil.

Emilia followed Bailey's lead, the beam of light was growing brighter. It filled her with hope. Hope that was sadly short-lived, as they approached the building they needed to be in, there was a wall of guards. They shared a knowing glance, before pulling out their weapons. Bailey asked for back up over the radio before they began their attack.

The two of them worked together, taking down the guards one by one by whatever means necessary. Emilia used her abilities to her advantage, dealing blows with spheres of steel blue, holding some of them in place while they tackled the ones closer to them.

"Emilia, look out!" Bailey shouted as he saw someone behind her, but before he had even finished warning her and arrow flew right into the side of his neck, taking him down within mere seconds.

Emilia smirked as she pulled the arrow from the downed soldier, passing it back to her friend.

"Thanks, Noah."

"You know me, always got your back." He said as he took the arrow back, immediately drawing it once again to fire at some of the remaining soldiers. It wasn't too long before they had wiped them all out and were able to proceed.

"It always seems to come down to us three, hey?" Noah tried to lighten the mood as they entered the building. There was an alarm blaring out around them.

"There will be more on the way," Bailey commented aloud. "We have to get moving."

The trio swiftly worked their way through the building, taking out the odd guard they came across. They just kept coming, though. Eventually they found the room where Amana and Matra were waiting for them.

"You guys alright?" Matra asked as he saw how flustered they were. The noise from the alarms going off above didn't seem to reach down here so the two appeared to be oblivious to the chaos. Matra quickly realised they weren't alone. "Oh."

Bailey and Matra did their best to fend off the guards but there was an abundance of them. It was as though for every one you took down, two more seemed to appear.

Thankfully, Noah was rather familiar with their systems having worked for an Agency for many years, and was currently in the process of overriding the door controls. If he could seal it shut, even if it was just for a little while, it would help immensely.

Over the grunts of pain, and the sound of bullets firing and steel meeting steel, there was an exclamation from Noah that turned some heads.

"Guys, I've got it. You need to get in here. Now!" He shouted over to everyone. Emilia was the first to get inside the room, after all, she was the one who needed to seal the gate. She had to be in. She used her abilities to force some of the close guards away so that Matra was able to make his way in.

"Bailey, come on!" Emilia shouted over the noise. Matra was providing covering fire, but the door was lowering, and Bailey was running out of time.

Bailey's ground hit the floor with a thud. As his back had been turned, the guards had taken the opportunity to turn all of their attention to him, not even phased by the gunshots coming from Matra.

"No!" Emilia screamed, rushing forward. She was restrained though, Noah wrapped her arms around her, stopping her from being trapped on the other side of the door. "Let me go! Noah, let go of me!" She screamed again and again, but she could do nothing but watch the door seal shut at the bottom.

"I'm sorry." Noah said in a quiet voice, guilt flooding him as he pulled her back away from the door. "We don't have time."

Noah's voice was overshadowed by banging on the door, countless soldiers firing shots at it trying to get in. Emilia sobbed as she stared at the door, knowing that not even Bailey would have been able to fight off the amount of guards that had followed them down.

The noise stopped after a little while, and Emilia tried to calm herself. Noah was apprehensive, and walked back over to the door, where he noticed that they were countering his deadlock. They were trying to open the door a different way after seeing that brute force wasn't the way to go. With alarmed eyes, he got to work in trying to keep the door sealed, shooting a panicked look over at Emilia before he started to command orders.

"Matra with me, you need to hold them off if they get through. Emilia, Amana, I don't know what you need to do, but you're going to need to get a move on! We still have company!"

Emilia took Amana's hand, leading her away from door, trying to feel for where the gate was. Amana took a deep breath herself, and with her hands she drew the outline of an arch. Steel blue lighting flickered, and like magic, it traced the outline of an archway, one appearing in the room before them.

The were exclamations of awe from Matra and Emilia, who took a moment to take it in. She stepped closer to it, trying to work out what it was exactly that she needed to do. Raising an open palm she tried pushing, tried sensing for any weak spots. The light around it brightened, casting a glow all around the small room. The outline started too shrink a little and Emilia let out a breathy laugh.

"Okay, we're getting somewhere." She stated, but she knew she was running out of time when she heard gunshots again. She put all her strength into it and it shrunk further, slowly closing and losing it's shape, but it was slowing down again.

A bad feeling overcame her, a nauseous feeling that started in her gut but quickly spread further, as she realised the crack in the gate didn't start in this realm, and could not be closed in this realm.

There were grunts of pain and the could hear how Noah was firing arrows as fast as he could. Without breaking her hold on the gate, she called him over.

"Noah." She called weakly, only one thing on her mind aside from saving her world. There was one person that she wanted to save the most. "There's too many of them, and I can't close the gate from this side."

"What?!" Noah's voice was abrupt, scared even. He never let up on firing arrows, but even they were finite and he would run out at some point. "We came all this way for nothing? You can't even close it?"

"From this side." Emilia corrected, a hint of sadness in her voice. Noah's eyes softened as he started to realise what she was saying, and they flickered to Amana, who looked terrified. "Keep her safe. Okay. Even if you have to go back to the mountains, forget all of this. Keep her safe."

Amana looked up at Emilia, and the pieces started to slot together as she realised the sacrifice that Emilia was about to make. The little girl shook her head, tears welling up in her eyes, trying to say no. Trying to defy her. Change what needed to be done.

"Amana, honey, listen." Emilia said, trying to keep her voice calm, steady, despite the shouting from Matra. They had no time to plan, discuss, she knew the soldiers would flood in here in seconds once Matra falls. "I need you to make a gate. Like you do when you're scared and want to get away from scary places, and I need you to take Noah with you. He's going to look after you, keep you safe. Aren't you, Noah?"

"I promise." Noah said, as he started to usher Amana further away from the door. "She'll be okay. I'll look after her."

There were shouts of protest from Amana, and tears were falling, but Noah took her hand, encouraging her.

"I know you will, Noah." Emilia's voice was quiet now. "Thank you."

Emilia could only watch them as they disappeared mere seconds later. Without Noah's arrows assisting him, Matra was overwhelmed with guards and the screams of pain were almost too much for Emilia to bear but she had to push on. She leapt through the small gap that was once a large archway, into the darkness of the unknown. It was easier on this side, where it all started.

Emilia saw the room she had just been in filled with guards, but it quickly vanished from view as the hole closed. She held her hands up for a little while longer, just to make sure it was truly closed and sealed off. Amana was safe, with Noah. Hopefully far away from Dalmaroi, somewhere safe and peaceful.

Exhausted, Emilia sunk down onto her knees, meeting the cold hard ground her emotions overwhelmed her. There was no one here, though. No one to comfort her, or judge her for the sobs that followed. The only thing that gave her comfort was knowing that Amana made it out of there. Emilia turned around, her back meeting what felt like stone where the gate had been just minutes ago. She pulled her knees up towards her chest.

The unknown frightened her, but she knew that she wasn't completely alone. This realm was the home to The Nox Malum, so it wouldn't be long until she had the pleasure to see them in person. They wouldn't be a mere folk tale myth anymore. They would be real, and Emilia didn't know if she had the power to survive them.

It was cold in here, wherever she was.

Cold and damp.

All alone.

Copyright © C. J. Pearce.

All rights reserved.

The story, all names, characters, and incidents portrayed in this production are fictitious. No identification with actual persons (living or deceased), places, buildings, and products is intended or should be inferred.

No part of this publication may be reproduced, distributed, or transmitted in any form or by any means, including photocopying, recording, or other electronic or mechanical methods, without the prior written permission of the author.

Book Cover by C.J. Pearce
2nd edition, 2025.

Printed in Great Britain
by Amazon